WE

ATOMIC RABBITS

Author and Illustrator

N.Protheroe

Published in Great Britain by
N. Protheroe,
Tyn-y-Bedw,
Llandre,
BOW STREET,
Dyfed,
SY24 5BZ

ISBN 0-9519840-0-4

Computer set in 11 on 11.5pt Bookman by
ARIOMA Editorial Services,
Gloucester House, High Street,
BORTH, Dyfed. SY24 5HZ

Printed by
Hollen Street Press Ltd.,
141/3 Farnham Road,
SLOUGH,
Berkshire,
SL1 4XB

Cover design by Patrick Smith Associates
Illustration by N.Protheroe

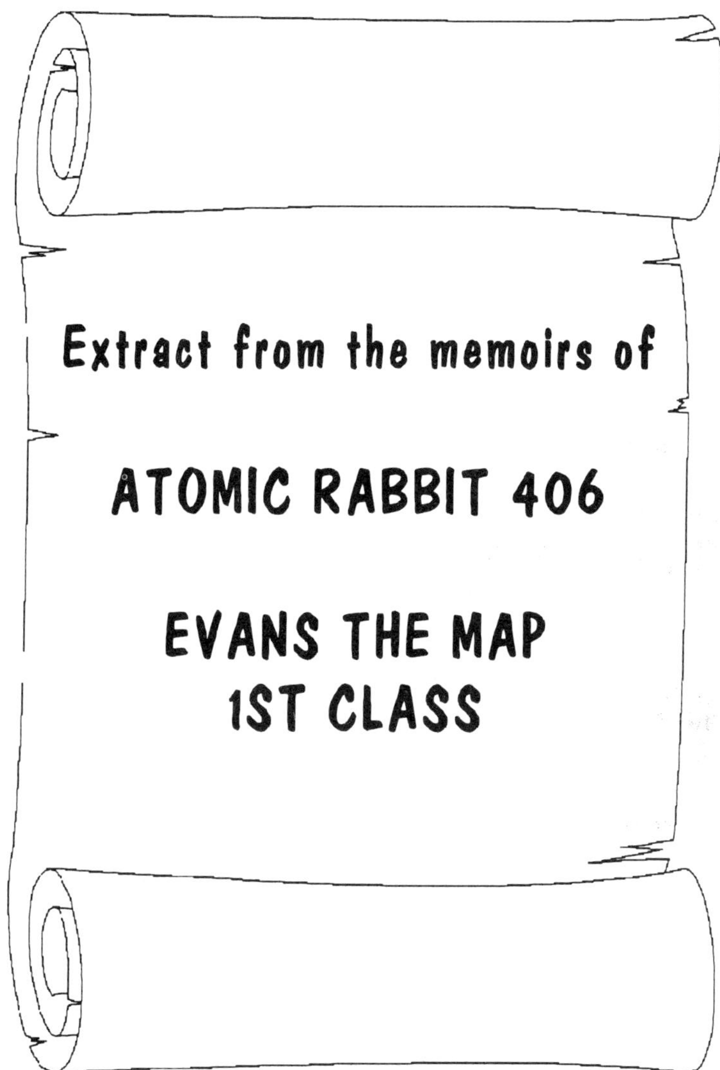
Extract from the memoirs of
ATOMIC RABBIT 406
EVANS THE MAP
1ST CLASS

ILLUSTRATIONS

EVANS THE
MAP.
N
E
S

Chapter One.

The secret army of Welsh Atomic Rabbits had been sent under the mountains of Wales, to undermine the foundations of English buildings, with the Atomic Power Station at Windscale as their first objective.

Dressed in wet-suits and flippers, to keep out the damp underground, they had been spotted by the S.A.S., who were now dropping sonar carrots down the holes, in a cunning attempt to capture them, but to no avail, as they had been very highly trained and, anyway, were on a strict cabbage and grapefruit diet. The only flaw spotted in their training so far was their habit of throwing the cabbage stalks up through the holes, which would account for the presence of the S.A.S.

Plan B would have to be put into action - a strategic retreat south for retraining, with special emphasis on parachute jumping down Wookey Hole, to get the troops used to the big heights they were to encounter later on. This they would do in the morning at 6 a.m.

At S.A.S. headquarters, a secret message had arrived, with the location of the Atomic Rabbits, so the S.A.S. would attack in the morning, at 6 a.m., just after dawn. It was a quiet, still night, and the Atomic Rabbits had a restful sleep, and were all packed and ready to move at five minutes to six. They formed up in a single file, and started for the surface; it was just a five-minute hop and walk up the passage to the daylight.

At S.A.S. headquarters, the men drew their thin, barbed cheese-wire stranglers from store, as this attack was to be a silent, head-lopping affair, done from behind, under cover of a single smoke canister. The S.A.S. made their way to the Atomic Rabbit location, arrived at the entrance to the hole at five minutes to six, and waited downwind.

The S.A.S. lay in the long grass and waited and waited and waited and waited, unable to understand why the Atomic Rabbits had not appeared.

The Atomic Rabbits, on the other hand, were now miles away, due to a great stroke of luck, as British Summer Time had started that night and the clocks had been put on one hour. The S.A.S. had put their watches forward, but The Atomic Rabbits had overlooked this, so had left one hour earlier.

At a top level meeting of Rabbit Atomic One, it was decided that holes would be cut in the wet suits, to facilitate a new breeding programme, to increase the number of Atomic Rabbits for the next dangerous mission. It was also suggested that the Atomic Rabbit Scientist, Taff One, should abandon his SOLAR TANK training in Snowdonia, as the mist and rain in this area tended to block out the sun and rust the metal bits. This could also be the reason why he had reached the summit of Snowdon once in eight years. This motion was carried with a unanimous show of paws.

The many dangers they were to encounter when Plan B was put into operation soon became apparent when Atomic Rabbit 406, Evans the Map, misread an English place name, and led them north to Barrow-in-Furness. However, this was spotted by their leader, who had spent a holiday there with a great aunt.

Plan B - part 2 - *Emergency Action Map-Reading Error* was now to be implemented.

The sundial was found to be lacking, and a compass was purchased. Atomic Rabbit 406, Evans the Map was sent on a two-week course (Extra Mural), to the Geography Department of Lancaster University, in order to become an expert in this ancient instrument. He went as a mature student, to allay the suspicions of the S.A.S., should they have an agent at the campus. Needless to say, Atomic Rabbit 406, Evans the Map, passed his exams with a first class pass and was duly awarded a scroll with green lettuce-coloured lettering.

So now no more journey errors were to be anticipated, and again the secret army was on its way to the correct map reference in the far south.

Leader also decided that flippers could now be removed, as speed was of the essence.

As soon as the sun rose that day they started their long journey south - packs on backs and flippers packed safely away.

Back at S.A.S. headquarters, the Boffins were working frantically on a Bionic Bunny, code-named Betty, with which they hoped to infiltrate the secret Welsh Atomic Army - unaware that, in Wales, Atomic Rabbits have not given equality to the female rabbits as yet. So, at best, Betty could only hope to reach the rank of private (Women's Branch), after successfully doing five years basic training.

The Atomic Rabbit Army was now making fairly good progress, and had covered a good 200 yards in the last hour, with just a short stop, for Atomic Rabbit 406, Evans the Map (1st Class) to re-check his compass with Magnetic North, and to wait for the pips on his wrist radio at eight o'clock.

After four gruelling hours, Leader called a rest stop - down at the bottom of a meadow by a small, bubbling brook. He duly unpacked the main bell tent and asked the other men to help him erect it, as it looked very much like rain. He estimated that the secret army had now covered three quarters of a mile.

Time now for a well earned rest, as they would make Lower Greenbank on the following day.

Leader, who was also the chief cashier, had made a boo-boo and mislaid the cash bag, which also contained his American Express Card, so he had asked his men if they had any readies he could borrow. They all looked deep down in their pouches and eventually produced the magnificent sum of 31p, which, if split between three, would not go very far.

After a long talk, it was decided that Atomic Rabbit 406, Evans the Map (1st Class) should get a job in a vegetarian restaurant in the evening, to secure some much needed finance. He would also be able to bring out any left-overs that might become available, therefore making the money stretch even further. But, tomorrow was another day - and the Atomic Three nodded off for the customary forty winks. It was at the thirty-ninth wink that they were aroused by a strange noise from without. Taff One was sent to investigate. As Leader said, if he had to do everything, then it was pointless being Leader - anyway, he didn't like the dark, as his ears tended to get caught in low branches.

Taff One gingerly lifted the tent flap, took one step out and tried to make out where the noise was coming from. There it was again - to the left, quite near, but high above him. He looked up, and there, at the top of the tree, was an S.A.S. Officer disguised as an owl, complete with yellow beak, big blinking eyes and sharp talons - fortunately for the Atomic Army, his parachute appeared entangled in the branches and he was stuck fast.

Taff One reported the facts to Leader, who, with his lightning brain, summed up the situation in a flash. They would leave him suspended there all night and leave early in the morning. With that they all got their ears down and nodded off.

Morning was five minutes late in coming, as there was quite a big hill to the east, which the sun had to climb. The Atomic Army cooked their breakfast, had a nice cup of tea with toast and marmalade.

Leader looked up into the tree; there was no sign of the S.A.S. man that Taff One said he'd seen.

Leader guessed that it probably was an owl, with a reflection of the moon on a cloud behind him giving the impression that it was a parachute, but he didn't tell Taff One, otherwise he might have wanted contact lenses - which he was always on about, and that would have used up the finances, which were not in a very healthy state anyway.

After breakfast, the Atomic Three packed away their utensils and tent, loaded up and set a course south by the map and compass of Atomic Rabbit 406, Evans the Map (1st Class). Their objective today would be to try and reach

Garstang.

First they had to pass through Four Ends Lane and Dolphinholme, and cross a bridge on the M6, in broad daylight; not an easy task for them to accomplish pushing a four-ton trailer, which they had found in a field. It had probably been used for silage a few short years ago, but the wheels still ran smoothly and it did gather a bit of speed going down hill, so sometimes they were able to sit on the back and sing songs as they went. It was a pity there was not one more of them, as then they could have formed a choir. Then again, this might have delayed them, as they probably would have had to attend choir practice twice a week, to get the piece they were singing up to standard, Atomic Welsh Rabbit Choirs being noted for their harmony.

They carried on pushing, and soon reached Garstang. They passed a vegetarian restaurant on the way, which had a card in the window that said, "Staff Wanted".

A black dinner jacket was purchased from the OXFAM Shop nearby for 2p, and it fitted Atomic Rabbit 406, Evans the Map (1st Class) down to the ground.

Leader obtained some Sellotape, and Atomic Rabbit 406, Evans the Map's (1st Class) ears were stuck down. The only thing which could ruin the disguise was his bobtail hanging out at the rear. So, to overcome this, Atomic Rabbit 406, Evans the Map (1st Class) would have to bow and leave the room backwards.

Atomic Rabbit 406, Evans the Map (1st Class) was successful at the interview and started the job immediately. The first customers were a bus full of Welsh Rabbits from the Rhondda, in South Wales, who enjoyed the meal and left Atomic Rabbit 406, Evans the Map (1st Class) a big tip. On the way out, they informed him that there were four spare seats on the bus, if they would like to go with them. Atomic Rabbit 406, Evans the Map (1st Class) telephoned Leader and told him of this. Leader said, as there were only three of them, it would be unwise to go on the bus, as this would leave one empty seat, which could arouse the suspicions of the S.A.S., hence making them an easy target for capture.

So Atomic Rabbit 406, Evans the Map (1st Class) duly

thanked the South Wales Rabbits for their kind offer, and said he was sorry that he could not accept it. They all gave him three cheers, and got on the bus, carrying a crate of dandelion wine.

At the restaurant on the following night, there was to be a folk evening, always popular with the local inhabitants, with one of the top northern folk singers, Ronnie 'Geordie' Rabbit, whose catch-phrase "Aawayhey man" had made him into an international star. It was a very busy night, and Atomic Rabbit 406, Evans the Map (1st Class), was rushed off his feet, but he didn't mind, as he also liked to listen to good music; anyway, with the lights turned down, he was able to walk about normally, and didn't have to bow and back out of the room every time he served someone. The highlight of the evening came with Ronnie singing that famous song "*A little fishy on a little dishy when the boot goes in*", which had been adopted by the Liverpool football fans as their club tune. Leader always said that, if there was time, they would go and see one of these strange functions, where twenty-three grown men kick a ball through three sticks, one way and then the other.

Atomic Rabbit 406, Evans the Map (1st Class) had a very busy night and was feeling a little pooped when Leader and Taff One called to take him back to camp in a taxi, which Atomic Rabbit 406, Evans the Map (1st Class), had to pay for.

Evans worked very hard every night for six weeks, giving all his pay and tips to Leader, who, apart from buying an essential portable colour T.V., to pass away the time while Atomic Rabbit 406, Evans the Map (1st Class), was working, had put the rest into the Bradford and Bingley Building Society, where it would gain interest.

A top level meeting of Rabbit Atomic One was called; all members were present. The minutes of the last secret meeting were read and found to be correct. These were voted on and accepted. Item one on the agenda was regarding the purchase of a tandem with a sidecar, which had been seen at the local garage only yesterday. It was proposed that Leader should negotiate the purchase of this valuable asset for as little as possible, which he agreed to do the very next day.

Down at the garage, the local hustler, who preferred to be called a sales manager, was putting the final touches to the tandem and hanging a price tag for £83, in bold red, on the handlebars.

Leader duly arrived to make the purchase, and as soon as he put his big foot in the forecourt, the sales manager appeared, like a weasel from a hedge. Leader glanced about, as if he was only there to ask the time, and this he duly did. It was fourteen minutes past twelve, which only left the sales manager forty-six minutes to lunch.

"Nice day," said Leader. Yes, it was, said the sales manager, who added, could he "be of any assistance?"

"Assistance for what?" said Leader.

"With the purchase of one of these fine, nay, superlative models, which have just this day arrived. Take, for instance, this ten-year old Morris 1000 with five thousand miles on the clock. Absolutely genuine. Belonged to a vicar's wife, who only used it to go to bingo on Fridays." Then, there was the superlative model of an Austin Maxi, a very sought after model and one which would not be in the saleroom for more than a day. Only twenty-eight careful owners, and had been maintained by this garage throughout its ownerships. Then, of course, there was the Ford Granada which would do forty-eight miles to the gallon, but needed a little attention to the bodywork, and that was the reason the price was so low....

Leader yawned and appeared to have lapsed into a trance. The sales manager looked at his watch - only another twelve minutes to lunch - and he tried to engage Leader in small talk. Had he been on his holidays yet? Where did he go? Did he enjoy himself? Where would he go next year? Was the food good? How did he travel there? Another furtive glance at the watch - only four minutes to go.

Leader appeared to be as uninterested as ever, when he casually strode past the tandem. The sales manager's hands were now nearly dry, when Leader turned and said, "It's been a very long time since I saw such an ancient mode of transport as this. But, could you tell me why the price is so high?"

"Probably an office error," said the sales manager.

"Oh!" said Leader. "What should the correct price be?"

"I'll go and check," said the sales manager, and did a quick flit into the building.

At three minutes past one he reappeared.

"Well," said Leader, "How much should it be?"

"Thirty-eight pounds," said the sales manager.

"I'll give you thirty," said Leader, "if you include Radar and a silent siren."

With lunch now uppermost in the sales manager's mind, the deal was done; Leader also asked for a discount for cash, which he received.

Leader went away happy, and the sales manager went away chuckling to himself, as he knew that the silent siren on the tandem did not work. Leader had no intention of using the silent siren in any case, as it might awaken the local inhabitants, if it were set off in the middle of the night.

Back at camp, Taff One had prepared lunch: a swede soup followed by spinach and lettuce salad, with grated carrot for afters, a rare treat. Leader rode into view on the tandem and sidecar, and all the members of the Secret Army cheered loudly; the journey south would now be a much easier affair.

After lunch, Leader had a quiet snooze while Taff One and Atomic Rabbit 406, Evans the Map (1st Class) did the washing up. Taff One washed up, and Atomic Rabbit 406, Evans the Map (1st Class) did the drying.

It was a pleasant, cool evening, and Leader said he would like to go fly-fishing, but the others pointed out that the bell tent would have to be erected in a safer place than last time. It was agreed that it would be better to erect it underground. One problem was how to get the big centre pole down the hole, as this bent at 45° to the left. Taff One said that the best thing would be to set off an explosive charge down the hole and, hopefully, the pole could then be lowered down the new hole. Leader was sent out to acquire some Plastic 8-0-8, which Taff One knew was very stable stuff, as he had once set alight to a stick, to boil a kettle and make a nice pot of tea, while on a summer holiday with a cousin on the River Calder, which ran through Towneley Park Golf Course, some twenty-four miles from Manchester.

Leader was not very successful and returned with a chemistry set, which he had bought at Woollies. Atomic Rabbit 406, Evans the Map (1st Class) had a shrewd idea what was going to happen next. Yes! He would have to enrol as a chemistry student, in order to become acquainted with the art of explosive manufacture.

"I'm fed up," he said, in a sudden burst of rabbit fury, hopping about and stamping his big left foot, which brought him around in circles, to confront Leader with this latest problem. "I'm not going to night school again," said Atomic Rabbit 406, Evans the Map (1st Class).

"Why ever not?" said Leader.

"I don't want any more qualifications than I have already, otherwise, I'll have to buy a bigger burrow to hang up all the certificates, when I get home."

"I understand," said Leader, with a tiny tear in his eye, "then Taff One will have to do it, as it was his idea in the first place." Taff One did not like the idea of night school one little bit, as he had a number of certificates as well. He was a trained whelk sniffer and cockle osteopath, neither of which skills had been called into use in the past five years.

Taff One introduced a counter measure, and called a top level meeting to discuss security, as this had got very lax in the past week. This was triggered off when Leader flagged down a bulk milk tanker by the M6 and asked for two pints, when everyone should have been aware that the Milk Marketing Board had gone metric, so Leader should have asked for a litre. He should also have carried an empty jug and not a brown paper bag, to facilitate a clean withdrawal back to camp, thereby alleviating himself of the necessity of licking up the trail of milk drops on the hard shoulder. Leader apologised for this oversight and promised that it was due to a lapse of concentration on his part, knowing full well that it was probably his age that had let him down - he'd noticed that his rabbit faculties were getting a little slower lately.

It was now nearly tea-time, and Taff One was looking forward to Welsh Sunday Tea, which, as everyone in Wales knows, consists of jelly, pears and ice cream, toast and a few lettuce sandwiches. The tablecloth was laid in the centre of a fairy ring, so they had a choice of toadstool chairs to sit on. They had just finished tea, when Leader noticed a lone cyclist heading towards them. He was coming across the field from the direction of the canal. Had the S.A.S. caught up with them?

Leader put the other members of the Secret Army on Red Alert; the cyclist drew nearer and nearer, until he was almost on them. He got off the bike and came into the fairy circle, he strode up to Leader and said, "Mon ami, would you like to buy some onions?" Leader glanced at the bike and noticed the string of onions right across the handlebars. He looked hard again at the stranger, he certainly looked familiar. Could it be - yes, it was - cousin Jacques, over from Brittany for the annual onion sale.

"Bon-Bon," said Leader, "I haven't seen you for some time, Jacques. Welcome to our secret camp. Please take a toadstool and have some tea, you must be very hungry after your long journey."

Jacques enjoyed his meal, and said that, if there was a night club in the area, he wouldn't mind going. Taff One reminded him that it was Sunday and everything would be closed, forgetting that this was England, and not Wales. Every Sunday, as far back as he could remember, he had been employed as a bouncer in the local Methodist Chapel. Leader said that he had heard there was a rugby club in the area.

"Don't be daft," said Atomic Rabbit 406, Evans the Map (1st Class), "they can't play rugby up here."

"That's why they have clubs," said Leader, "to try and learn our sport." He had heard that they had managed to master the ancient chant of Ogi, Ogi, Ogi-Ogi, which was a start in the right direction.

That night, the carrot juice flowed like water, and Taff One was the first to go under, but before he hit the floor he managed to do a traditional clog dance with broom and candle.

"Why the candle?" Atomic Rabbit 406, Evans the Map (1st Class) asked later.

"You should know that," said Leader. "It's so you can see the exit doors if the performance becomes boring, and you want to leave in a hurry." What with Atomic Rabbit 406, Evans the Map (1st Class) hitting the floor, and Taff One and Leader being the worse for wear, nobody had noticed Jacques leaving early by the side door.

When time was called, the Secret Army mustered themselves together for the walk back to camp. It was then that Leader noticed that Jacques was missing. They looked under the table and in all the ashtrays, but failed to find him anywhere. It was a clear, moonlit night, and the cool air helped to clear the heads of the Secret Army as they walked back to camp. The question remained, why had Jacques disappeared and what had happened to him? When the Atomic Army reached camp, the only trace of him was an empty bike and two cycle clips - where was Jacques and where were the strings of onions? It would be many weeks before the Secret Army were able to solve this mystery.

In the meantime, the Secret Army played the last post, switched their light out, and fell asleep almost where they stood.

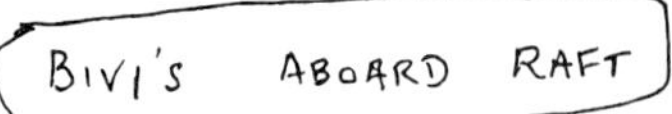
BIVI'S ABOARD RAFT

SWAN TO THE RESCUE

Chapter Two

The S.A.S. had had a great stroke of luck and managed to capture Jacques as he left the Rugby Club. He was now being interrogated as to the whereabouts of the others. Although very willing to talk, as he had drunk a little too much of the carrot juice, the only thing he had said so far was, "Mon ami, would you like to buy some onions?" In fact, this was the only thing they were likely to get out of him, as this was the only phrase he knew. As they said back in Brittany, "He may not be a great conversationalist, but could he sell onions!"

Jacques started to chat away in Breton, which none of the S.A.S. men could understand. Thinking it was a coded message, they set about writing everything down and trying to decode it. They took his beret off his head and tried to find the maker's mark, looking for the slightest clue which might betray the Welsh Atomic Rabbits' headquarters. Yes, there was a label inside. It was pretty dark now, but they could just make out some letters. Where was the light? "Back in stores," said one. "Has anyone any matches?" said another. Yes, Big Mack had a box.

Big Mack came forward, took out the matches and struck one - fizzle-fizzle - it went out; he tried again and again and again, but they all went the same way. Big Mack was now down to his last match. He struck it. It lit up, but in their haste to read the label the beret fell to the floor, and the light from the match was now used to find it. It was found, and just as the label was about to be read the last match went out, too. They would now have to wait until daylight before the beret revealed its secret.

Morning arrived, and as the first rays of light came up, the beret was brought forward. The label could now be seen clearly - what did it have to say? - A coded message, no less: *Six and seven eighths, hand wash, made in Taiwan*. The S.A.S. despatched this message to headquarters for the boffins to work on. Jacques, in the meantime, had sobered up and was drinking a cup of lemon tea he had been offered.

The Secret Army had a lie-in that morning, each hoping that one of the others would rise first, get a fire started, put the kettle on and make an early morning cuppa. Leader feigned sleep, snored and turned over. Atomic Rabbit 406, Evans the Map (First Class) was asleep, which left Taff One to do the honours.

He picked up a dry stick and some sphagnum moss, found a rough stone and started to twist the stick between his paws and the stone, having first placed a piece of moss where the stick and the stone rubbed against each other. A small puff of smoke appeared, Taff One blew gently on the moss and it caught fire. He added more moss and a few dry sticks, which were lying around, and soon the fire was crackling away. He picked up the kettle and went down to the stream for water. When he returned, he could see that the fire was really going, and had set alight to the field of stubble where they had been camping. He hoped that Leader and Atomic Rabbit 406, Evans the Map (First Class) were safe. He called out to them in the secret way that he had been taught. He got the wind behind him, then he cupped his paws over his mouth, took a deep breath and shouted, "Atomic Rabbit 406, Evans the Map, where are you?"

"We're standing behind you," said Leader. "How many times have you been told not to play with fire? Now look what you've done. The field's on fire, the cows are running and there's a big red lorry with a ladder on top heading this way. Jump in the sidecar, Taff One, while Atomic Rabbit 406, Evans the Map (First Class) and I pedal you out of this mess."

In he popped, full kettle and all, and away they went, pedalling towards the sun, as they now realised from what Atomic Rabbit 406, Evans the Map (First Class) had told them that this was the south, and he should know, as he was the one who went to night school. Off they went. It was a nice, sunny day, and the miles started to melt away; it was then that things started to go wrong. A wobble started in the nearside wheel, which carried the sidecar; water started to splash out of the kettle, and Taff One got wetter and wetter. Leader pulled into a lay-by on the side of the road, to see what the trouble was. Taff One got out of the sidecar; he looked more like a wet mop than an Atomic Rabbit. Leader knelt down and looked under the sidecar. The nearside drive-shaft coupling had broken, and this would now have to be replaced.

"Ring around the local garages," said Leader, "to see if they have one." Atomic Rabbit 406, Evans the Map (First Class) went off to look for a telephone kiosk. He walked three miles before he came to one which, unfortunately, had been vandalised. He had started to walk back when he remembered that he had passed three garages on his way to find the telephone. He would call at these on his way back, and ask in person for the replacement part. The first garage he called at did not have one in stock, but could order one, which would probably take three days to arrive. He thanked them, but declined to place an order. The second garage had the part required, but the mechanic had just gone to lunch and would not be back until two o'clock.

"That would be fine," said Atomic Rabbit 406, Evans the Map (First Class). "It will give me time to go back to the lay-by and return with the tandem." Off he went, and as he was passing the next garage he noticed that Leader and Taff One were just coming out, riding the tandem, which they had managed to get repaired.

"How much did that cost you?" asked Atomic Rabbit 406, Evans the Map (First Class).

"Not very much," said Leader, "as the part was one which had been in stock for a number of years. Even the price list had to be dusted off. The part was listed at three shillings and seven pence. The garage owner was able to convert this to 85p decimal, plus fifteen per cent V.A.T., which brought the total to ninety-eight pence."

Leader had paid the invoice and told the manager to keep

the change. Atomic Rabbit 406, Evans the Map (First Class) now got into the sidecar, although the seat was still wet where Taff One had spilt the water, but it made a nice change to see others doing the work, and to just sit and enjoy the scenery. It was very flat from Garstang, and they had soon pedalled down to Bilsborrow; another ten miles and they should be at Preston. Leader confirmed this with Atomic Rabbit 406, Evans the Map (First Class), who agreed with this observation and, anyway, all the signposts they passed said so.

After another two hours pedalling, and some excellent steering by Leader, they pulled into the grounds of the local park. Leader said they would spend the night there. Due to their hurried exit from the last camp site, they were now minus the big bell tent and they would have to revert to pitching two small bivouacs, which were in the sidecar of the tandem. It was now getting quite dark, so they hurried to find a suitable place to pitch for the night.

Leader found a nice, square, flat piece of ground, which had some rings fitted into the surface. "Great," said Taff One. "We'll just fix the guy ropes to the rings; that will save a lot of bother trying to hammer pegs in this hard ground - and also cut down on any noise the mallet would make."

The wind was quite strong that night, and the piece of ground they were camped on trembled from the gusts which blew. Daylight came, and they had a nice lie-in. Leader was the first to crawl out of the bivouac. He looked around, blinked and then blinked again. "Oh, no!" he said to himself. "How am I going to explain this to the others?" All he could see, in every direction, was water. They were camped on a raft, which must have come free from its moorings, and now they were in the middle of a lake, becalmed, as the wind had dropped. He crawled back into the bivouac. Taff One was still asleep in the corner. He crawled out again and untied the string on Evans the Map (1st Class)'s bivouac. Atomic Rabbit 406, Evans the Map (First Class) was just waking up, and he was quite surprised to see Leader there, and thought that it must mean an early morning cup of tea.

"No, it's not a cup of tea," said Leader. "It's a small problem, which will have to be resolved before we can proceed any further."

"What is it?" asked Atomic Rabbit 406, Evans the Map (First Class).

"You're not going to believe this," said Leader.

"Tell me, anyway," said Atomic Rabbit 406, Evans the Map (First Class).

"Well, when you chose the camp site last night, we camped on a raft, and now we have drifted out on it into the middle of a lake."

"Oh, dear," said Atomic Rabbit 406, Evans the Map (First Class), "what will Taff One have to say when he finds out!"

"We had better resolve the problem before he does," said Leader.

They had a big think, but think as they may, the problem was no nearer to a solution when Taff One popped his head out of his bivouac. "Good grief!" he exclaimed. "We're out at sea."

"No," said Leader, "I think it's a lake."

"It's water, anyway," said Atomic Rabbit 406, Evans the Map (First Class).

Taff One now had a think. "I know," he said. "We'll take the sidecar off the tandem, put up a bivouac pole, use a bivouac canvas for a sail and head out until we see land."

"What a brilliant idea," said Leader. "Why didn't I think of that?"

"A small problem," said Atomic Rabbit 406, Evans the Map (First Class). "Where are the tandem and sidecar?"

"What do you mean?" asked Leader. "You had them last night."

"Well, last night, I leant the tandem against a tree, and I suppose it's still where I put it."

"Oh, dear," said Taff One, "I'll have to think again."

Two hours later they were no nearer to an answer to the problem. Not only that, but they were now getting a little hungry, and the food and cooking gear were stowed neatly away in the sidecar. Taff One's belly started to rumble as pangs of hunger got worse and worse. Still, there was no wind on the lake, and it was now getting nearer to tea-time.

"I know," said Leader. "We'll take a plank out of the raft and use it as a paddle."

All the planks on the raft were nailed tightly in place and, tug as they might, nothing could be budged. Just as they were giving up all hope, a swan alighted on the water next to them.

"What do you think you're doing on my lake?" he asked. Leader did his best to explain, and the swan believed him.

"I'll help you out this time," he said, "but don't let it happen again."

With that, he picked up in his beak the end of a rope, which was tied to the raft, and started to paddle for the distant shore. The journey took them about an hour, and they were towed to the very spot where the tandem had been left.

"Great! great! great!" exclaimed Leader. "I'll make us all a big dinner."

Swan said he didn't want anything cooked, but would be very pleased if he could have some pieces of bread, as this would sustain him on his flight south east to the River Thames for the annual Swan Upping.

Leader looked at him as if he knew what he was talking about and wished him luck on his flight south, anyway.

They gorged themselves at dinner until they were hardly able to move. They would have been very easy targets for the S.A.S., had they attacked then, but the S.A.S. were busy drilling Bionic Betty in all the arts of Atomic Rabbit training, and she was very near to the completion of her very exacting course. In fact, she only had to learn the art of dressing in traditional Welsh costume, to be a very acceptable member of Welsh society. Even in England, they prized a good Welsh dresser, fully laden, which Bionic Betty certainly was.

It was a Saturday, and the day had been set aside for the

big passing out parade for Bionic Betty. The Commander-in-Chief of the S.A.S. would be there for the march past. Who would be in the band for this special occasion, as none of the S.A.S. could play any instruments?

The Commander-in-Chief said, "We had better put an advert in the national papers."

"We can't do that," said the Adjutant, "as we are supposed to be an incognito organisation."

"I didn't mean that the advert should say that the band was needed for the S.A.S. Just put 'Band required, to train men in marching to music'". This was agreed, and the advert was duly placed in *The Times* and the colour supplement of *The Observer*.

The Atomic Army lay down in the long grass and had a long, long, long snooze, after their ordeal on the raft. Yet another meeting of Rabbit Atomic One was called, and Leader took the chair as usual. All the formalities were observed: reading the minutes, voting et cetera. Then it came to any other business. Leader suggested that a torch be purchased, as the nights were getting dark. It would also help in the siting of future camps, as he did not want to spend any more time stranded in the middle of any more lakes. The motion was unopposed and, therefore, carried.

Tomorrow was Sunday, and another special day in the lives of the Welsh Atomic Rabbits. It was Atomic Rabbit 406, Evans the Map (First Class)'s birthday, and the Secret Army were going to go all out to celebrate this very personal occasion. Leader set about hiring a hall and booking some entertainment. Food and drink were laid on, and all that was wanted was for Sunday to arrive. As it was Atomic Rabbit 406, Evans the Map (First Class)'s birthday, Leader said that he could make the breakfast, as a special treat. Then, after breakfast, he could design some posters, and put them up in prominent positions around the town. Leader would sell the tickets at the door, and Taff One could be the bouncer, as he had great experience of this post from back home.

"Shouldn't we hold a raffle?" said Atomic Rabbit 406, Evans the Map (First Class), whose birthday it was.

"It's a good idea," said Leader, "but what will we offer as the prize?"

"I know," said Taff One, "a week's holiday with my sister Blodwen in Porthcawl."

"I didn't know your sister lived in Porthcawl," said Leader.

"She doesn't," said Taff One, "but she's always wanted to go there, and this seems a golden opportunity not to be missed."

"I'd hate to win that prize," said Atomic Rabbit 406, Evans the Map (First Class).

"Why?" enquired Taff One.

"Well, you see, Taff One, I'm one of the few people to have seen your sister Blodwen in broad daylight, patches of fur falling out and a large pimple on her left ear."

"She's better now," said Taff One. "She was only in that condition because she was allergic to dandelion stalks."

"How much should we charge for the entrance fee tomorrow night?" asked Leader.

"Oh, I think it should be kept as low as possible, then we'll sell more raffle tickets," said Atomic Rabbit 406, Evans the Map (First Class). "It would be no use charging a high entrance fee, as then very few people would attend, so the raffle tickets would not be as popular to buy."

It was agreed that the entrance fee be fixed at ten pence and that the raffle tickets should be twenty pence. They all washed and changed into their best clothes. Taff One got into his evening jacket, which he had used in the restaurant, Leader donned a polo-necked sweater, knitted for him by his mother two Christmases ago, and Atomic Rabbit 406, Evans the Map (First Class) looked very handsome indeed in white spats and monocle, which he only wore for very, very special occasions. They were all ready for the big day to arrive, but first - early to bed, as the special day would be very hectic indeed.

At S.A.S. headquarters, the parade ground had been prepared with a dais, for the Commander-in-Chief to review the parade. Bionic Betty marched and counter-marched, quick-marched and slow-marched, and presented arms as she passed close to the dais. It was a very impressive display and she was duly awarded the coveted Welsh Hat with accessories, which included a spare set of batteries.

Sunday morning arrived, and Atomic Rabbit 406, Evans the Map (First Class) was up very early and had produced a number of very attractive and eye-catching posters, which were placed in all the best positions in the town, and gave the venue and the inclusive menu, all for twenty pence.

In fact, this event was likely to be a sell-out, as the population of Preston knew a bargain when they saw one. The hall was full to overflowing and the food was devoured in the first half hour. Everyone sat back to enjoy the entertainment. First came the dancers, with their acrobatic movements, then a magician, who made people levitate and then turned them into rabbits and made them disappear into a top hat. The highlight of the evening was the appearance of a huge cake with candles flickering, which was wheeled onto the middle of the stage. Atomic Rabbit 406, Evans the Map (First Class) was invited on stage to blow out the candles.

He was carried shoulder high from the back of the hall to the stage, to the strains of *Happy Birthday to You, Happy Birthday, Dear Atomic Rabbit 406, Evans the Map (First Class), Happy Birthday to you.* Atomic Rabbit 406, Evans the Map (First Class) thanked all those assembled for their very kind gesture, and took a large breath, in order to blow the candles out in one go. He turned to face the cake, to a fanfare of trumpets. He blew on each candle in turn, and they went out one after another, all except the one in the middle, which, try as he might, refused to go out. Eventually, Atomic Rabbit 406, Evans the Map (First Class) came to the end of his patience, and he pulled out the candle. As he did so, the top of the cake burst open and up popped a female rabbit dressed in pink feathers, with her long eyelashes fluttering. It was Bionic Betty of the S.A.S. and in her paws she held a sub-machine gun, the M.K.5, which could fire three hundred rounds per minute, and she was pointing it straight at Atomic Rabbit 406, Evans the Map (First Class).

"You are under arrest," bleeped Bionic Betty in her

transistorised voice. "Turn around and walk slowly towards the Exit Door."

The audience loved this unexpected spectacle, and clapped and cheered, not knowing that Atomic Rabbit 406, Evans the Map (First Class) had been taken prisoner.

After the show was over and all the money had been counted, Leader said that they would have to carry it in the sidecar of the tandem. Then they would try to find out how the S.A.S. had known that the Atomic Army would be present in the hall.

Leader called an Atomic Army meeting, and the two members were present. Question one was how this unpleasant action had happened, and on Atomic Rabbit 406, Evans the Map (First Class)'s birthday as well.

"Better start at the beginning," said Taff One. "Who knew of the event? Well, that's easy; everyone knew because of the posters."

"Well, let's see what gave our presence away," said Leader.

Taff One obtained one of the posters, and there on the bottom was the evidence, "Tickets for sale at the door, or obtainable from any member of the Atomic Rabbit Army".

"So that's how they knew," said Leader. Well, now there were only two of them, so extra care would have to be taken to avoid any more slip ups. Question two was where had they taken Atomic Rabbit 406, Evans the Map (First Class)?

"Let's start from where we last saw him," said Leader.

They went back to the stage and looked into the empty cake, something glistened at the bottom. Taff One climbed inside to examine it closer.

"What is it?" asked Leader.

"It looks like a drop of oil," said Taff One.

"There's another on the floor out here," said Leader, "and another by the exit door."

Could it be that Atomic Rabbit 406, Evans the Map (First

Class) had left a trail for the Atomic Duo to follow?

"It might be a trap," said Leader, "but as this is our only clue, we shall have to follow it, but this time with great caution."

The trail led them along the pavement, then across the road, down a dark alleyway and to a disused aqueduct, which had been turned into lock-up garages. It was at the one with the big green door that the oil suddenly stopped. Muffled voices could be heard inside, if a jam jar were to be placed against the door and an ear placed against the jam jar.

They listened very quietly, but could not make out what was being said. There was a small scraping noise on the gravel behind them. They spun around and, to their horror, were confronted by Bionic Betty and her machine gun.

"Hop this way," said Bionic Betty. "I have somebody whom you would like to meet - albeit for the last time."

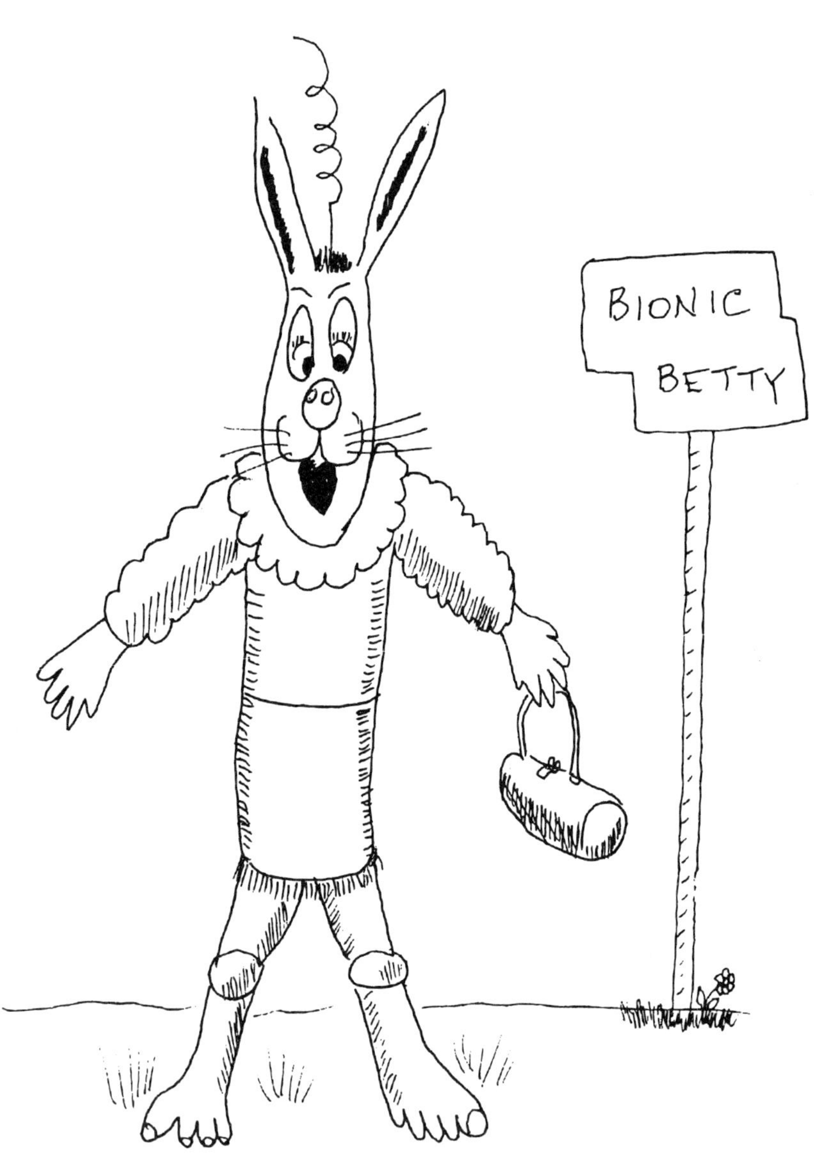
BIONIC
BETTY

Chapter Three

Leader gave Taff One a downcast glance as they were ushered through another entrance, next but one to the green door. It was dark and damp inside, the only light came from a small, flickering candle on a box in the corner.

Against the wall, they could make out the slumped figure of Atomic Rabbit 406, Evans the Map (First Class). Leader was ordered to tie up Taff One, which he did, as he had learned to tie knots while in the wood-craft section of the Scout pack, of which he had been a member when he was a lad.

Bionic Betty ordered Leader to place his paws behind his back, which he duly did. Bionic Betty tied him up very tightly and placed him and Taff One with Atomic Rabbit 406, Evans the Map (First Class), against the wall. They were there all night. At dawn, Bionic Betty threw open the doors of the garage, and the light flooded in, to reveal the Atomic Army in a very sorry state. Bionic Betty ordered the Atomic Army to turn around. She asked them if they had any last requests before she exterminated them. Taff One could not think of anything at the moment, but said that if he was given time he was bound to think of something. Atomic Rabbit 406, Evans the Map (First Class) said that he would like to learn to use a sextant so that the Atomic Army, had the circumstances been different, would be able to travel at night. Leader said he would like to smoke a last Havana Havana cigar, one of the big, fat Crown ones.

Bionic Betty thought for a moment and then said that she was sorry Taff One could not think of anything, and that she would not be able to grant Atomic Rabbit 406, Evans the Map (First Class) his request, as she did not know of anyone in the district who could operate a sextant. Leader's request she could grant, as there was a tobacconist at the end of the street.

"How much does a Crown Havana cost?" she asked.

"About eight pounds," said Leader, "but I only have two pounds in my purse. We have some money hidden away in the sidecar of the tandem, back at the hall."

"I'll go and get it," said Bionic Betty. "You can hold the gun and guard your two friends, but first I'll have to untie you."

She duly did this, and handed the gun over to Leader.

"I'll be about ten minutes," she said and, with that, she went off towards the hall.

Leader waited until she had gone round the corner before frantically setting about untying the other members of the Atomic Army. He was also very surprised to find that Atomic Rabbit 406, Evans the Map (First Class) was fast asleep against the wall, and was not really paying attention to anything. Leader shook him gently and said, "We had better try to reach the tandem and sidecar before Bionic Betty gets there."

Off they set, at full hop, as Bionic Betty had a good half minute's start on them. They reached the tandem first and hopped on and into the sidecar, and started to pedal south as fast as they could. They stopped at the junction with a roundabout, to let Bionic Betty through on her way to the hall. They all gave her a wave, and she was able to wave back, as she passed them going down a one-way street with all her indicators flashing.

"That was a very narrow escape," said Leader.

"Thank heaven you like to smoke cigars," said Atomic Rabbit 406, Evans the Map (First Class).

"It certainly is," said Taff One," although I don't like the smell of them and the smoke tends to cling to the upholstery in the burrow."

"When we get home, I'll try and install an air purifier in our burrow," said Leader.

"That would be very nice," said Taff One.

They had cycled about six miles before they suddenly realised that they had not eaten since that last fateful meal in the hall. Leader apologised to Atomic Rabbit 406, Evans the Map (First Class) for such a bad start to his birthday celebrations and hoped that he was not too disappointed, as it was the thought that counted anyway. Taff One said, "That was a good idea of yours to lay that trail of oil for us to follow, Evans."

"What trail of oil," asked Atomic Rabbit 406, Evans the Map (First Class).

"You know," said Taff One, "the one from the hall to where you were tied up."

"That wasn't me," said Atomic Rabbit 406, Evans the Map (First Class). "It must have come from a leak in Bionic Betty."

"That's what I call a real stroke of luck," said Leader.

They journeyed on in relaxed mood until they came to a sign which read *Clayton-le-Woods*.

"This sounds a nice place to stay for a while," said Leader.

"We must not stay too long," said Taff One, "as the S.A.S. cannot be far behind, and are probably plotting our route this very moment."

Back at S.A.S. headquarters, Bionic Betty was being taken apart to be reprogrammed. This time, she would not take any notice of traffic lights, or other street sign posts like one-way streets.

A nice field appeared to the left, and Leader steered the tandem and sidecar into the field and started to unpack the cooking utensils. Atomic Rabbit 406, Evans the Map (First Class) said he would cook the meal. After eating and doing the washing-up, Leader called an extra special meeting of Atomic Rabbit One.

Important decisions would have to be taken to safeguard the journey south to Wookey Hole of the Secret Army. Should they stick to the chosen route, or should they have a diversion, to put the S.A.S. off the scent?

"I suggest that we double back to where we started out, and start out again," said Taff One.

"That's the daftest idea I've ever heard," said Leader.

"I agree," said Atomic Rabbit 406, Evans the Map (First Class). "What would be the point in starting again, especially after purchasing a compass?"

"I think we should catch a bus," said Leader.

"We can't do that," said Taff One. "How would we get the tandem and sidecar up the stairs? Anyway, where would we catch a bus to?"

"I know," said Atomic Rabbit 406, Evans the Map (First Class), "we'll catch one that goes south."

"What a dumb thing to say," said Taff One.

"Oh, if you can think of anything better, then let's hear it," said Atomic Rabbit 406, Evans the Map (First Class).

"All this bickering is getting us nowhere," said Leader. "Let's have a good think about it and then, possibly, we will find a solution."

Atomic Rabbit 406, Evans the Map (First Class) failed to find any more ideas relevant, or irrelevant, to the situation. Taff One had a look of blank amazement written all over his face, and even his ears went down to a new low. It looked as if the master plan would have to be devised by Leader, who suddenly had a brain-wave and said, "I think I've got the answer."

"What answer?" asked Taff One, who was getting more bored as the seconds ticked by.

"The answer," said Leader, "to our problem."

"Oh, good," said Atomic Rabbit 406, Evans the Map (First Class). "I find all this thinking saps my strength."

"We'll go by canal," said Leader.

"I would have thought that our last trip on water would

have cured you of any thoughts of this nature," said Taff One, "but it is a good idea, all the same. It will be less hectic than pedalling the tandem and sidecar, and we would be able to relax for quite a distance between locks."

"Oh, we're going by barge," said Atomic Rabbit 406, Evans the Map (First Class).

"Certainly," said Leader.

"Oh, good. I've always wanted to ride a horse," said Atomic Rabbit 406, Evans the Map (First Class).

"What has that got to do with anything?" asked Taff One.

"I'm afraid there won't be a horse to ride," said Leader.

"How are we to propel the barge, then?" asked Atomic Rabbit 406, Evans the Map (First Class).

"It will have an engine," said Leader.

"I don't know if I can come with you, then," said Atomic Rabbit 406, Evans the Map (First Class), who added, "I have terrible trouble stopping my ears from going limp."

"Don't make a fuss. You can stay on deck for the whole journey," said Leader, "then the fumes won't reach you."

"That's all very well," said Atomic Rabbit 406, Evans the Map (First Class), "but what happens if it rains?"

"You can put your wet-suit and flippers back on," said Taff One. "Anyway, it's about time you took those spats and that monocle off; they may have looked nice in the hall, but now it looks as if they need a good stint at the cleaners."

"You don't send monocles to the cleaners," said Atomic Rabbit 406, Evans the Map (First Class), "and, anyway, you whiten spats."

"Do keep quiet," said Leader, "while I try and think where we can hire a barge."

"Why not try walking on the canal bank?" said Taff One, "then we are bound to come to a garage for barges."

"They don't have garages for barges," said Leader. "They have wharfs."

"I thought wharfs were those plastic things holding a fishing rod they put beside wishing wells in a garden," said Atomic Rabbit 406, Evans the Map (First Class).

"You would," said Taff One. "What would we do on a barge down a wishing well, except go round and round in circles?"

"Please try and think of something constructive to say to each other," said Leader, "or we are going to be stuck in this field forever."

"Well, let's get on the canal bank for a start," said Taff One.

Off they set once more, on the tandem and sidecar, pushing it onto the towpath.

"Well, here we are at last. Which way do we go now?" asked Taff One.

"Let's consult the compass."

"Which way do we go now, Atomic Rabbit 406, Evans the Map (First Class)?

"Well, according to the compass, we go straight across the canal," said Atomic Rabbit 406, Evans the Map (First Class).

"That can't be right," said Leader. "You must be holding it too close to the tandem."

"I'll move further away then, and take another reading," said Atomic Rabbit 406, Evans the Map (First Class). "You were quite correct," said Atomic Rabbit 406, Evans the Map (First Class). "I must have been standing too close. According to the new reading, we have to travel in that direction," he said, pointing south.

"Which canal are we on?" asked Taff One.

"It's the Leeds and Liverpool Canal," said Leader, "and that's what the sign you are leaning on says."

Well, they took turns at pushing the tandem and sidecar, and eventually they came to a lagoon, where there was a number of barges for rent.

"Who said it was a wharf?" asked Atomic Rabbit 406, Evans the Map (First Class). "It's a lagoon."

"Never mind what it is," said Leader. "We had better find out how much the rental is."

"There's an office over there," said Taff One. "Let's go over and see."

"It's thirty-five pounds a week, if you hire it for a week and then bring it back here. If you take it up to the next lagoon and leave it there, it will only cost fifteen pounds a week," said the owner.

"We'll take it for the week and leave it at the next lagoon," said Leader.

The transaction completed, they loaded themselves and the tandem and sidecar onto the barge. The owner of the barge showed them around the craft, and pointed out all the important bits, so that they should have no difficulty in sailing it. He showed Leader how to start the engine and how to operate the tiller. Then he left them to their own devices.

Leader started the engine, and the barge shuddered but didn't move.

"We don't appear to be going anywhere," said Taff One.

"We would," said Leader, "if you cast off the painter at the stern."

"There's nothing worse than a know-all nautical rabbit," thought Taff One. He untied the rope at the stern and the barge began to glide along, and they all gave a great sigh of relief. Atomic Rabbit 406, Evans the Map (First Class) was appointed chief cook and placed in charge of the galley, in spite of the fact that he said he suffered from headaches when he breathed the fumes. But Leader felt that he would be much too busy making tea and other meals, and when he wasn't doing the cooking there would always be the washing up.

Leader held the tiller and did quite a good job steering the barge. The Atomic Rabbits were soon very much at ease on the barge, and things were ticking over quite well. Cups of hot tea would appear from the galley every hour. Taff One returned the cups when they were empty, and Atomic Rabbit 406, Evans the Map (First Class), Chief Cook, did all the washing up, and came on deck very occasionally with a damp tea towel, which he would tie to the side rails to dry. It was now getting dark, and Leader suggested that they moor the barge for the evening.

They found a nice, quiet stretch of water, where trees grew on either side of the canal. Leader stopped the engine and steered the barge to the canal bank. Taff One took the painter and secured the barge to a handy tree at the stern, and secured the bow to a bough which was growing at a handy height. It was a very peaceful evening, with fish making a plopping sound when they jumped out of the water, trying to catch flies. A few elegant purple and green dragonflies hovered over the water, and water boatmen skipped here and there on top of the water.

"I wonder how they manage to walk on the water like that," said Taff One.

"I think they have inflatable feet," said Atomic Rabbit 406, Evans the Map (First Class) Chief Cook - who had now appeared on deck with another tasty snack.

"Rubbish," said Leader. "It's because they have very hairy feet that don't break the fine skin on top of the water, so they don't sink to the bottom."

"How do you know all these things?" asked Taff One.

"Oh, because I used to pay attention when I was sent to school," said Leader.

"I wish I had listened more closely," said Taff One, "but I couldn't seem to keep my mind off carrots for more than two minutes at a time."

"I used to dream of them as well," said Atomic Rabbit 406, Evans the Map (First Class) Chief Cook, "but I tried not to think of them until playtime and again after school. That was probably the worst time, when we were training at Atomic Rabbit Headquarters, and I had to forget about them and shift my allegiance over to cabbage and grapefruit."

"Yes, we all suffered then," said Leader, "but it helped us

escape being captured by the S.A.S. at Windscale."

"That's very true," said Taff One.

"Don't you think it's time we contacted Atomic Rabbit Headquarters for further orders?" suggested Leader.

"Oh, I don't think that would be a very good idea just now," said Taff One. "It might give away our position to the S.A.S. and we are enjoying our quiet trip on the canal."

"Anyway, let's get below and turn in for the night," said Leader.

They all climbed down the ladder and battened down the hatches. Atomic Rabbit 406, Evans the Map (First Class) Chief Cook found a hammock stowed away in one of the lockers, and proceeded to hitch up the ropes to the bulkhead frames. He put a pillow at one end and threw a blanket in, then he jumped into the hammock. The hammock received him willingly, then it changed its mind and deposited him back on the lower deck, faster than the wink in a lizard's eye

"Woops!" said Taff One. "You had better have another go."

The repeat performance was as interesting as before, except that there was a double back flip incorporated into this journey from the hammock to the deck. The pillow and the blanket remained where Atomic Rabbit 406, Evans the Map (First Class) Chief Cook had placed them.

"I've always wanted to have a go at sleeping in a hammock," said Taff One. "Give me a go."

Taff One climbed up and settled down nicely. "There, that's how it's done," said Taff One, "easy peezey." He turned to fluff the pillow and, lo and behold, the hammock tossed him firmly but gently into the air, and from there back down onto the deck.

"Easy peezey!" said Leader. "I think you two would be better off sleeping in my diddy bag."

"I think I'll sleep in that bunk over there," said Taff One, nursing a newly acquired bruise and wondering to himself - what was a diddy bag?

"Good night," said Leader, as he turned down the Tilley lamp. The Atomic Three were soon fast asleep and dreaming of all the nice things that only rabbits can dream of.

Morning arrived, to find it raining quite heavily on the canal. Taff One was all for staying snug and warm in his bunk all day. Atomic Rabbit 406, Evans the Map (First Class) Chief Cook said he'd better get up, or he would have no breakfast. Leader smiled to himself, as he knew that Taff One was very partial to the first meal of the day. Taff One gave a big yawn, as he rolled out of his bunk and plopped into an upright position.

"Lead me to it," he said. "I've been quite hungry for the past two hours."

Again Atomic Rabbit 406, Evans the Map (First Class) Chief Cook did them proud. Chickweed and dandelion salad, served at just the right mixture, as he had been trained to do when he worked in the kitchens of an hotel in Pwllheli in his younger days.

The rain had stopped, and although there was no sun, it did manage to get dryer and warmer. Leader started the engine, and Taff One cast off 'fore and aft', as they say in sailing circles, or back and front, as they say in Rabbit circles. The barge moved smoothly through the water, passed under a bridge and rounded a turn in the canal. There, ahead of them, was a lock, and nearby stood the lock keeper's cottage and the general store, which had a post office combined.

"That's handy, Leader," said Taff One.

"Never mind that," said Leader, "let's get the barge through the lock gates as quickly and efficiently as possible."

"Always giving orders," thought Taff One, "and never a moment to contemplate the wonders of nature, but what can you expect from someone with his background? Even his burrow, back home, was on the wrong side of the hill."

Leader steered the barge into the lock and Taff One turned the lock gate wheel until the gates were closed behind them. Then the water began to rise very slowly. While all this was happening, Atomic Rabbit 406, Evans the Map (First

Class) Chief Cook suddenly appeared from below and gave a mighty hop on to the towpath, then he took two more purposeful hops and disappeared into the shop.

"Funny bunny," thought leader, "he doesn't have any money and yet he's gone shopping. There must be a free offer. Typical of a Cardiganshire Rabbit to know about it before anyone else, though." But Atomic Rabbit 406, Evans the Map (First Class) Chief Cook hopped past all the shelves containing the goodies and hopped up to the post office counter, where he looked the post mistress straight in the eye and said, "Is there anything for me?"

"What's the name?" asked the post mistress.

"Atomic Rabbit 406, Evans the Map (First Class) Chief Cook," said Atomic Rabbit 406, Evans the Map (First Class) Chief Cook.

"I think I've seen that name recently," said the post mistress. "Yes, here we are, a letter from Bargoed - well, that's what the postmark says."

"Oh, that's from my Aunty Flo in South Wales," said Atomic Rabbit 406, Evans the Map (First Class) Chief Cook.

"I'm afraid there will be eight pence to pay," said the post mistress.

"I'll have to pop out to the barge to get it," said Atomic Rabbit 406, Evans the Map (First Class) Chief Cook. He hopped outside and went over to the barge, which had now risen halfway up the lock. Could he have eight pence, he called to Leader.

"Whatever do you want eight pence for?" asked Leader.

"It's to pay excess postage on my letter," said Atomic Rabbit 406, Evans the Map (First Class) Chief Cook.

"What letter?" asked Leader.

"One to me from my Aunty Flo in South Wales," said Atomic Rabbit 406, Evans the Map (First Class) Chief Cook.

"Oh, no! Not from your Aunty Flo. She really must stop looking into her crystal ball to see where her favourite nephew is. She must be made to realise that her clairvoyant gifts must not be used like that. It is a breach of the secret code of the Atomic Army to have your Aunty Flo know where you are at any given time," said Leader.

"I'm very sorry, but can I have the eight pence, so I can have my letter? I'm dying to find out what she has to say," said Atomic Rabbit 406, Evans the Map (First Class) Chief Cook.

"Oh, I suppose so," said Leader, "after all, you did work in that Restaurant for six weeks." Leader went below and returned with the eight pence and gave it to Atomic Rabbit 406, Evans the Map (First Class) Chief Cook, who dashed back into the shop and went up to the post office counter, which now had a closed sign above the grill.

ON THE CANAL
LEADER

LEADER!

Chapter Four

"Oh, Hoppy-de-de! I'll come back after tea," said Atomic Rabbit 406, Evans the Map (First Class) Chief Cook. Back he hopped to the barge, to explain the situation to Leader, who was even more interested to find out what Aunty Flo had to say.

The barge had now risen to the correct level in the lock, and Taff One was busy turning the wheel, to open the gates, to let the barge out onto the new stretch of canal. The barge was moored, and they settled back to yet another nice meal of watercress and wild angelica, sprinkled over with chopped wild celery. After a quiet snooze, taken to the accompaniment of the lapping of water against the side of the barge, they awoke refreshed and all were now more eager than ever to find out what Aunty Flo had to say.

"Never mind the washing up," said Leader, "go and get your Aunty Flo's letter."

Atomic Rabbit 406, Evans the Map (First Class) Chief Cook flew along the towpath like a dose of salts, and into the shop. He emerged three minutes later, clutching the letter in his paws, and made his way back to the barge.

"What does it say?" asked Taff One.

"I don't know," said Atomic Rabbit 406, Evans the Map (First Class) Chief Cook. "I haven't managed to open it yet. Aunty Flo has stuck it down with Sellotape."

"That, if you will excuse me saying so," said Leader, "is one of the more annoying aspects of your Aunty Flo. Remember last Christmas, when she sent you that card -

that was all stuck down, too. It took us until Easter to open it and then, when we did, it was an Easter card with the message *Happy Easter. I knew you would not manage to open this for Christmas. Love, Aunty Flo.*"

"We should manage a lot better this time," said Taff One. "We have a good knife aboard the barge."

They all went below and set about opening the letter. It took around five minutes to find the knife and to cut through the Sellotape - but, at last, the job was done. Atomic Rabbit 406, Evans the Map (First Class) Chief Cook took the pages neatly in his paws and started to read to himself.

"Read it out loud," said Leader, "then we'll all know what she has written."

"Yes, please do," said Taff One. "I, for one, can't stand the suspense any longer."

Atomic Rabbit 406, Evans the Map (First Class) Chief Cook took a deep breath, gave a little cough to clear his tubes and started by saying, "Mr. Chairman (Leader) and fellow members of the Atomic Army (Taff One), it gives me great pleasure to read out the contents of Aunty Flo's letter to you all.

"Please get on with it," said Taff One.

"He's doing his best," said Leader.

"Well, here goes," said Atomic Rabbit 406, Evans the Map (First Class) Chief Cook. "It's addressed to me."

"Of course it is," said Leader, "otherwise, the Post Office would not have known who to deliver it to."

"Please let him get on with it, Leader," said Taff One, "otherwise, we'll be here all night.

"Continue," said Leader.

"The letter starts, *Dear Ploppykins*".

"Dear who?" said Leader.

"Dear Ploppykins. It's what Aunty Flo calls me," said Atomic Rabbit 406, Evans the Map (First Class) Chief Cook.

"Well I never," said Taff One, starting to chuckle and hold his paws on his tummy. He rocked to and fro on his hind paws. Leader started to chuckle, too, and before very long they were both laughing and rolling about on the deck.

"Well, if that's your attitude, I'm not going to read any more," said Atomic Rabbit 406, Evans the Map (First Class) Chief Cook, alias Ploppykins. An hour passed, as Taff One and Leader rolled about helplessly on the deck, tears of laughter formed pools here and there and the pain in their bellies got worse all the time. At long last, they managed to pull themselves together and were again able to sit upright.

"Please go on," said Leader. "Taff One and I are very sorry to have interrupted you with your letter."

"I'll skip the introductions this time and get down to the nitty gritty of the letter," said Atomic Rabbit 406, Evans the Map (First Class) Chief Cook alias Ploppykins, and continued to read the letter.

I'm glad that you and your two friends have escaped the attentions of the S.A.S. and of that Bionic Betty. I was only telling your mother last week, and we both agreed that the three of you had better keep well clear of her, as she only means trouble for you. Blodwen from the village sends her regards, and reminds you of the nice time you both had at the last burrow picnic.

Old Uncle Tom has gone to live in the Old Folks' Burrows, as his eyesight is getting worse. The Reverend Idris Pritchard ordered the churchyard to be cleared, so all the rabbits at Top Burrow end now have a short cut down to the brook. The ladies section of the Farm Bunnies Union have been on a trip to Glastonbury for the Summer Solstice, but it rained, so nobody saw anything.

The local paper, The Burrow, *has again had to raise its charges, so your mother and I are going to buy one every other week and pass it on to each other. You know the old saying,* Save the acorns and the oak trees will look after themselves. *There has been a good lot of mushrooms this year, so your Uncle Edgar has put on a lot of weight and your Aunty Maud has made him go to keep-fit classes.*

The local rabbit commune have been out collecting the magic mushrooms, and they held their annual Rainbow Festival again, but this year they were invaded by a group of punk rabbits, and the local Hare Police had to run them in. They can move quite fast when they want to.

Your father has been seeing that Enid at Bracken End Lane; your mother doesn't know, so please don't let on that I told you. Your elder sister has set up home with Ebenezer Fluff, so it looks as if you might have a lot more relatives in a very short time. Anyway, the Atomic Army could do with more recruits. Well, I think that's all for now. See you at the Mill on the twenty-eighth.

Best of luck, watch you don't catch cold, best wishes,

Aunty Flo.

"Well, you read that very well," said Leader.

"Hear! Hear!" said Taff One. "But, what did she mean 'see you at the Mill on the twenty-eighth?'"

"I really don't know, but being the clairvoyant that she is, I suppose we will see her then," said Atomic Rabbit 406, Evans the Map (First Class) Chief Cook alias Ploppykins.

"But what mill and which twenty-eighth?"

"I don't know, so we will have to wait and see."

"It's time we cast off and got under way," said Leader. "It will soon be getting dark."

Taff One cast off once again and the barge slipped quietly forward. Atomic Rabbit 406, Evans the Map (First Class) Chief Cook alias Ploppykins did the washing up and started to prepare the evening meal.

They came to four more locks and passed through without incident. Four other barges passed them, going the other way, then the light began to fade. They moored the barge again and settled down for a peaceful night. Another morning, another day, not far to go now for the next lock, but first, the best meal of the day, as Taff One would say. Nothing moved inside the barge, except for Taff One's empty tummy, and his patience was now coming to an end.

"Uhu hoo, Ploppykins, time to get up and make the food."

"I'm not getting up, so you will have to make it yourself," said Atomic Rabbit 406, Evans the Map (First Class) Chief Cook alias Ploppykins.

"Everyone to his duty," said Leader. "Taff One is chief cast-off barge operative, so I'm afraid you will have to get up."

"Well, I never," said Atomic Rabbit 406, Evans the Map (First Class) Chief Cook alias Ploppykins. "If I'm chief cook and Taff One is chief cast-off barge operative, what might your function on this barge be?

Leader thought for a while, then he said, "I'm leader and captain of this vessel, with other duties, such as chief purser, coupled with other duties, like engineer and others which do not readily come to mind.

"That should teach you to ask questions," said Taff One, "so, you had better rise and shine, so that the rest of us can sit and dine."

"Oh, all right, I suppose I'll have to get up then," said Atomic Rabbit 406, Evans the Map (First Class) Chief Cook alias Ploppykins.

After breakfast and the washing up, all members of the Atomic Army mustered on deck to listen to Leader, to find out what the new plan of action was to be when they left the barge and took to the country once again.

"Well, fellow members of the Atomic Army," started Leader, "at this very moment, I do not have any firm plan of action for when we leave this barge, which has been our home for the past four days."

"What are we going to do, then?" asked Taff One. "Do we just hang about on the towpath with the tandem until the S.A.S. capture us and cart us away to one of their ghastly, secret prisons, never to be heard of again?"

"Don't be stupid," said Leader. "I would not allow that to happen, it would mean that his Aunty Flo would put the 'fluence on me."

"She would too," said Atomic Rabbit 406, Evans the Map (First Class) Chief Cook alias Ploppykins. "You just remember what she did to Willy Wobbly, in the village back home, when he refused to buy one of her raffle tickets."

"What was that?" asked Taff One.

"It's hard for me to say what she did exactly, but he was never able to ride his bike in a straight line ever again."

"I do wish you two would stop talking about the S.A.S. and your Aunty Flo, especially your Aunty Flo," said Leader. "You know they make me uneasy, and that gives me indigestion."

"Well, I do hope you come up with something soon," said Taff One.

"I will, I will," said Leader, "just give me a little time. Well, we had better get under way, or we will never manage to reach our retraining area, and we must get there before the winter starts to set in. Cast off for'ard, cast off aft."

Taff One did this - as soon as Leader gave the order, and the barge slipped on quietly once again through the still, quiet water of the canal, with only the rippling of the water and the gentle murmur of the trees and rushes, as the breeze passed through them, to listen to. They came safely through the last lock and on to the lagoon, where the Atomic Army disembarked and handed over the barge to one of the men at the wharf, who was wearing a black, peaked sailor's cap. He thanked the Atomic Three for looking after the vessel and for the professional way they had sailed her.

The Atomic Army checked over the tandem and re-inflated one of the tyres, which had lost a bit of pressure. They took a compass reading, looked at the map and set off once more on their journey south. But first, they had to cycle to a quiet, safe spot, to pitch the tent for a night's rest.

Eventually, they came to a bridge, which ran over the canal; a small humped bridge with a narrow road passing over it. One side had an ancient arch, which ran parallel to the canal, and set into the arch were two small openings which opened onto two small rooms, which themselves opened onto each other on the inside.

"I think this is the spot for our camp," said Leader. "Nice and sheltered, with a place to stow the tandem out of sight, and also a place to cook our meal under the shelter of the arch." It looked very much as if a storm was on its way.

Taff One pushed the tandem out of sight, and was heard to grunt and heave; he reappeared carrying the tent, and set about putting it up as a canopy over one of the entrances to the arch.

"That's a good idea," said Leader. "It will stop the rain blowing in when the storm starts."

Leader had no sooner finished when the sky went suddenly black and large spots of rain started to splash down, making the Atomic Three scurry for shelter. It was quite dry under the arch, and after the meal, they settled down for a good night's rest, and to stay dry until the storm had blown and splashed itself out. They spent a very restless hour trying to nod off, but to no avail, as the thudding of the raindrops seemed to hit the ground and create and echo inside the arch where the Atomic Three were sheltering. Forks of lightning lit up the sky, followed by loud claps of thunder, which made their ears fold down over the sides of their fluffy heads.

"I hope it will pass soon," said Leader, who, underneath his strong personality, was wobbling like a blancmange on the Sunday dinner plate. The noise of the storm grew nearer and nearer, with more and more flashes of lightning, and the crashes of thunder now seemed to be directly overhead. A great flash came out of the sky and seemed to hit the tent pole, which was holding the canvas over the entrance; smoke came from the canvas, but because it was wet it failed to ignite.

"That's the first bit of luck we have had today," said Taff One, from the safety of a blanket pulled over his head, in the furthest corner of the arch. Large spots of rain, the diameter of a football, fell from the sky, but inside the arch all was dry. The water swirled past the doorway in quite a strong current. The Atomic Three closed their eyes, curled up and went to sleep, hoping for a better day.

Dawn broke with the sound of birds wishing each other

good morning to musical accompaniment, as only they can. Song thrushes passed the chorus from one tree to another, female blackbirds with brown plumage strutted up and down the lane, and turned over fallen leaves, in the never ending search for juicy worms. Linnets chatted away to chaffinches, and yellow beaked starlings, dressed up in their evening dress suits, chatted to everyone that would listen.

Ploppykins was the first to open an eye, and what he saw made him feel that all was well with the world. The sky was clear and the sun's rays were hitting every tree, bush and blade of grass, and made them shine and shimmer as they dried out.

"I don't really mind being called Ploppykins," thought Atomic Rabbit 406, Evans the Map (First Class) Chief Cook. "I must bring it up at the next meeting of Atomic One, then perhaps we might make even more progress towards our goal in the South."

Taff One and Leader woke up together, looked at each other and both said, "What did you say?" Both gave the same reply, "Nothing."

Ploppykins said, "Good morning," but was greeted by two loud grunts in reply. "I won't try that again," he thought.

Leader got out the maps and asked for a compass bearing, which he duly got.

"Today, we will make an early start," he said, "to avoid any trouble from heavy traffic."

Taff One pointed out that the time was already ten o'clock, but, undaunted, Leader said the early start would have to be made at a delayed time. How could you argue with that, thought Taff One. After all, he was the Leader.

"Shall we hold a meeting of Atomic One?" asked Taff One.

"Let's get going first," said Leader.

The tandem was wheeled out and the sidecar was packed up with all their vital equipment. They all clambered aboard and set off down the road at a brisk pace, not too fast, as they all wanted to enjoy the lovely countryside. They pedalled for two hours, and found it quite easy, as the land was very flat. Leader spotted a lay-by and steered the tandem to a smooth halt. They all got down and started to search for fresh plants, to make a nice meal. Taff One tried to find dandelions, so that he could put them in a jam jar to brighten up the table. Butterflies sailed about in the gentle breeze, going about from one flower to another, sucking up the nectar and covering their noses in pollen. A big yellow and black-shirted bumblebee droned lazily about, sometimes missing the flower he started out for, but he didn't seem to mind a bit.

"I've found some salad burnet," said Leader. "I like to crush the leaves and add it to the spring water, as it makes a cooling summer drink."

At last, Taff One arrived with an armful of dandelion with a smothering of rough hawkbit. Evans the Map was late, as he always was on these occasions, but at last he plopped out of the hedge with some ground elder and some sorrel.

"That should do it," said Leader, and with that, everybody set to, and the beautiful salad was ready in the blink of an eye. After the meal had been eaten and the spring water with the added garnish had been drunk, nobody wanted to do anything but lie back on the grassy bank and snooze in the sunshine. Leader was the first on his feet, and as he yawned, he noticed a sign that was nailed to a tree branch; it read, "Ye Olde Mill. Cream Teas, 200 yards on the left."

"Oh, no," said Leader quietly to himself, "not Ploppykins's Aunty Flo. I couldn't face a cream tea, but if I don't mention it, perhaps they won't notice the sign."

Taff One stood up and gave Evans the Map a dig in the ribs.

"Look up there," he said. "Cream Teas 200 yards on the left."

"But we have just eaten," said Ploppykins.

"Never mind," said Taff One. "Perhaps we could have one next time we see a sign."

"That will be something to look forward to," said Leader, thinking to himself that it had been a close shave.

Again the tandem was prepared and the Atomic Three mounted and started off once more, but they hadn't travelled 200 yards when they ran over a broken milk bottle, which punctured the front tyre.

"Oh, dear, we seem to have a puncture," said Taff One, as always, stating the obvious.

"I know where the bottle came from," said Leader. "There's a pile of bottles here in the hedge."

"A cow's nest, I suppose," thought Taff One.

"Well, that's gone and done it," thought Leader. "Any minute now and Aunty Flo will appear on her broomstick."

"We had better hold a meeting of Atomic One," said Taff One.

What on earth for?" asked Leader.

"To plan our course of action," replied Taff One.

"Oh, very well," said Leader, "where are the minutes of the last meeting?

"You had them last," said Evans the Map.

"No, I didn't," said Leader.

"Does it matter who had them last?" asked Taff One. "Where are the secret papers now? Better look in the tandem." And so they did, and, at long last, found them in the drawer marked '*Secret Papers*'.

"Good," said Leader. "I thought they might have fallen into the hands of our enemy, the S.A.S."

"Order! Order! Order!" said Leader. "This special meeting of Atomic One is in session." The minutes of the last meeting were read and were accepted by the members present.

"What shall we have on the agenda this time?" asked Leader.

"I should like to have my name shortened," said Atomic Rabbit 406, Evans the Map (First Class) Chief Cook alias Ploppykins.

"What do you want it shortened to?" asked Taff One.

"I don't want such a long name, that's all," said Evans the Map.

"Well, let's make a list of possible names," suggested Leader.

"How about Twitch, or Sniffkin?" said Taff One.

Leader suggested Longy, or Wigley, but Evans the Map didn't like any of them.

"What would you like to be called?" asked Leader.

Atomic Rabbit 406, Evans the Map (First Class) Chief Cook alias Ploppykins thought for a while and then came out with, "How about Evans?"

"What a good idea," replied Leader. "Let's take a vote on it, then."

"I vote for it," said Evans the Map.

"So do I," said Taff One.

"Just a second," said Leader. "Is that a proposal and a seconder?"

"I think it is," said Taff One.

"Goody, goody, goody," said Evans. "I'll be known as Evans. Well, now that's over, what next?"

"What next! How about a quick repair of the tyre on the tandem?"

Evans was very relieved that his name had been changed; now he could put messages on the cards he sent to Aunty Flo, instead of just writing his name. There might even be room to make a little drawing. Aunty Flo would like that - she had quite a good collection of scrapbooks containing cards with drawings on them. "I'll pump up the tandem," he thought. "Leader and Taff One will like that."

He pumped and pumped, but still the tyre was flat. "It looks as if I'll have to mend the puncture before we are able to continue our journey," he thought. Evans found a bandage and proceeded to wrap it around and around the tube, and he finished off the job with a nice, big bow. He pumped again, and lo and behold, the tyre stayed up. There was just one small snag: the bandaging would not pass through the fork.

"Oh, snookered again, eh!" said Leader.

"Afraid so," replied Evans.

"You'll have to buy another wheel," said Taff One, yet again stating the obvious.

Two buses passed, one contained a crowd of football hooligans on their way to spend a night in the cells, and to miss the match at the same time. The other bus contained Aunty Flo, on a shopping trip to Altrincham Market with her friends, hoping for yet another bargain, but mainly to use up her council travel passes before they expired.

"That reminds me," said Leader, "we must sell the portable T.V. set, to avoid paying the licence fee. Anyway, the detector van must not be allowed to find the location of the Atomic Army, and a court appearance would do us no good at present, not to mention a write-up in the local paper."

It was now the beginning of June, with the smell of hay and silage being cut, and hay fever in the air, as the pollen count seems to shoot up at this season. On the path, an army of ants trudged, all in line and all in step, on their way to build and scale another ant hill. But first, they had to make base camp, to arrange their strategy for the assault on the summit. Why they keep doing this is anybody's guess, as they never take photographs of their achievements, or stick a flag on the summit. But that's ants for you; always going places and getting nowhere.

"They are a bit like us," thought Leader, "for we appear to be doing the same at this moment."

Yet another meeting of Atomic One was called, to test the morale of the troops and to plan the next move for the Atomic Army.

"I suggest we make tracks for Offa's Dyke, so that we can then proceed south in more or less a straight line," said Evans.

"Is that a firm proposal?" asked Leader.

"It is," said Evans.

"Well, can we vote on it then."

"Perhaps there are other suggestions," said Taff One.

"Well, what are they?" asked Leader, wondering if the meeting would ever end.

"I think we should go to Offa's Dyke," said Taff One.

"I wonder where he got that idea from," thought Leader.

"That sounds like a good idea," said Evans, not being one to drag another down.

"Let's vote, then," said Leader. "Those in favour - Taff One. Those against - Evans. It looks as if I have the casting vote, and I vote in favour."

"Taff One's motion carried," said Evans, "but only by a majority vote."

This was duly entered in the minutes of the Secret Army. Then it was time for a dandelion coffee brew; (the root had been dried and grated by Aunty Flo, 'which,' she said, 'was common practice in the early nineteen-forties.')

"I wonder how old Aunty Flo is," thought Leader. "She seems to have so many recipes and remedies at her paw tips."

It started to rain heavily, and Taff One was seen hopping into the sidecar of the tandem.

"That should be reserved for me," thought Leader.

Evans got back into his wet suit and flippers, and didn't seem to mind the downpour.

"Do you remember when we three trained to be frog-bunny-men at the amphibious frog-bunny warfare centre at Poole?" asked Evans.

"I'd rather not go into that," said Leader.

"When they asked Taff One if he would like to canoe," said Evans, "and he said that he would, and the very next thing was that he had to carry a canoe across the mud flats for three miles."

"I have never volunteered to canoe again," said Taff One.

"I should think not," said Evans. "They never did find that canoe."

"How was I to know that the tide was going out?" asked Taff One.

"Easy peasy, you should have consulted the tide tables," said Evans.

"What's a tide table?" thought Taff One. "I've heard of coffee tables and breakfast tables, even dinner tables, but never tide tables."

"Please cut out the bickering," said Leader, "or we'll never reach our re-training area at this rate."

"Time for big eats," said Evans, who was looking forward to having a full tummy again.

"Shall we have a surprise today?" suggested Taff One.

"Yes, let's," said Leader. "I saw a very attractive Italian restaurant a while back. Let's go there. I think that the readies will cover the expense.

The rain had stopped and Mr. Sun was shining everywhere. They reached the restaurant and went inside. They were greeted by a very flashy Italian rabbit waiter named Bertoldoni Bertoline Pasquale Smith.

Chapter Five

"*Scusi*", said Leader, "*butá doyá havá spinaci insalate for three?*"

"*Si, tre spinace insalate*," said Bertoldoni Bertoline Pasquale Smith, as he disappeared into the kitchen.

"Where did you learn to speak such fluent Italian?" asked Evans.

"Quite easy, really," said Leader. "I used to frequent an Italian family, and I picked it up from them."

The spinach salads were brought, and Leader asked, "*Quanto?*" and Bertoldoni Bertoline Pasquale Smith replied, "That will be five pounds *in totale*." Leader gave him a fiver and a ten pence tip.

"*Mille grazie*," said Bertoldoni Bertoline Pasquale Smith. "*Buona sera.*"

"It can't be night already," thought Leader, "but, I'll let his error pass this time."

All three left the restaurant, and hopped up and down on the pavement, avoiding the cracks in the flagstones, until they arrived back at the tandem. The next task on the agenda was to get a new wheel for the tandem, then they had to unwrap the bandage from the old wheel, and replace it in the first aid box, washed first, of course, as everything in the box had to be kept hygienic.

"I suggest we have a quick nap," said Taff One, who was always ready to put his nose on the ground and his tail in the air.

"We can't sleep now," said Leader. "We have much to do to get the unit into peak fighting condition, both physically and mechanically."

"I'll remove the wheel from the tandem," said Evans.

"And I'll undo the bandage," said Taff One.

"I suppose that means I'll have to wash it," said Leader.

"You suppose right once again," said Evans. "It must be quite exciting to be able to be correct about most things."

"That, said Leader, "is why I'm Leader.

They walked to the nearest village, to see if they could obtain a wheel, but all that the village contained was an undertaker and sport shop in one.

"Strange kind of shop to have in a village," said Taff One.

"I think it is a good idea," said Evans.

"However do you come to that conclusion?" asked Leader.

"It's handy for those who kill themselves with that new-fangled jogging," said Evans.

"I suppose you're right," said Leader. "If people were supposed to jog, then they would have been born as horses."

"What's a horse," asked Taff One, who had never seen a horse at close quarters.

"It's one of those things that looks like a cow, but it doesn't have horns," explained Evans.

"I still don't know what it is," said Taff One. "If it hasn't got horns, what does it have?"

"It has a bell, of course," said Leader.

"Why didn't you say that in the beginning?" asked Taff One, "then, we would all know what you are talking about. It is a donkey substitute. I've been on one of those, when we used to go to the seaside on holiday, when I was much younger and carefree - before the time when I was trained to be in the Atomic Army."

"Ah! Heady days," said Leader, a tear in his eye. He

turned away and quickly wiped away the tear, so as not to embarrass his two friends, who looked up to him as Leader.

"Evans, where are we now?" asked Leader.

"We are here," said Evans.

"I know we are here," said Leader, "but where is here in relation to a point on the map?"

"To tell you the truth, I haven't the foggiest idea where we are," said Evans.

"All that training and all those exams you sat, and you don't know where we are!" said Taff One.

"If you persist in asking me stupid questions, Leader, then I shall give a stupid answer," said Evans.

"I only asked where we were," said Leader.

"Well, if you look up, you will see that we are under a signpost, and if you look down, you will see that you are sitting on a milestone."

"I should have twigged that," said Leader.

"You see, you don't have to go to night school at all, or to pass exams, really, do you?" said Evans.

"You do, if you want to be an Atomic Rabbit," said Taff One.

"Good heavens!" said Evans, "he has made a statement all on his own; things are really looking up."

"We have managed to travel some thirty-six miles from Garstang, according to this milestone," said Leader.

"Yes, but which way are we going?" asked Taff One.

"It's south, according to the map and my trusty compass," said Evans.

"Well, if that's the case," said Leader, "we'll be lucky to reach Offa's Dyke, never mind the re-training area at Wookey Hole."

"There's something fishy going on. By my reckoning, we must be a lot further south than this," said Evans.

"How do you mean," asked Leader.

"Well, can you remember the trip on the canal? We travelled a good distance on the boat," said Taff One.

"I think I'll climb up that wall to see if I can see any obvious landmark to check against the map," said Evans.

"Good idea," said Taff One.

Evans clambered up and was able to sight a church spire and a very tall chimney stack.

"I thought so," said Evans, and as he said it, he slipped and fell, scratching both his paws against the wall.

"You'll have to have those bandaged," said Taff One.

"I will. They are starting to sting already," said Evans.

"Look on the bright side," said Leader, "you are now the only Atomic Rabbit with his own double-grazing."

"Very funny. Very funny," said Evans, who thought that in an emergency there is nothing funny about a funny bunny. With both his paws bandaged, he had difficulty in unfolding the map, but at last he managed it.

"I thought so," he said. "We are near Preston."

"Are you sure about that?" asked Leader. "If you are, then how do you explain the milestone and the signpost?"

"I think that the S.A.S. have planted them, to confuse the Atomic Army." said Evans.

"I don't think that is very likely," said Taff One.

"We had better hold a meeting of Atomic One," said Leader.

"I agree," said Taff One, who was always ready to sit down and have a chin wag. The meeting was duly held and all were present.

Leader opened up with, "Where the dickens are we?"

"I second that," said Taff One.

"That was a question, not a proposal," said Leader.

"I second that," said Evans.

"Can we please get down to the nitty gritty of this meeting," said Leader, "and would you two stop seconding everything that I say."

"We both second that," said Evans and Taff One.

"I suggest that we book the three of us on one of those day trips going south, to see how far we can get in a day," said Leader.

"What a splendid idea, but what about the tandem and sidecar?" asked Evans.

"We'll just have to pick a trip with plenty of room in the boot of the bus," said Taff One. "This lad is really coming on," he thought. "As nobody else would think it, I must."

"I saw a notice board outside that shop in the village," said Leader.

"What did it say?" asked Evans.

"It said, *Day Trip to Gretna - £3 return.*"

"Brilliant observation, Leader, especially when it's going in the opposite direction to that which we want," said Taff One.

"Was that the only trip advertised?" asked Evans.

"No, there were others," said Leader, "but not as interesting as the one to Gretna."

"Well, what were the others?" asked Taff One.

"One was to see the lights of Leamington," said Leader.

"I see what you meant about interest," said Evans.

"Then, there was a trip across the Mersey to New Brighton," said Leader.

"Is that the lot?" asked Evans.

"Oh, there was one other," said Leader, "a day trip to the Llangollen International Festival, but that's in the first week in August, and that's three weeks away."

"Let's go to that thing in Llangollen, it will give us a good start for a final push to Offa's Dyke," said Evans.

"But, what on earth are we going to do for three weeks, while we wait for the trip to come?"

"I've thought about that, too," said Leader. "We are all overdue for a period of leave, so it would be a good idea to have it now."

"What a jolly wheeze," said Taff One, who prepared himself for a visit to an uncle who lived in London.

"Where will you go, Evans?" asked Leader.

"Oh, I think I'll take it easy and rest my weary body and mind from all the rigours of the Atomic Army. I think I'll go to Betws-y-coed. I've heard that it's very nice there at this time of the year, with the sun glinting off the slate quarries in the early dawn."

"Doesn't sound very exciting to me," said Leader, "but everybody to his own thing."

"We had better take a six figure map reference now," said Evans, "so that we can all meet here in fifteen days time."

Leader issued three leave chits for the members of the Atomic Army, who received them and destroyed them, as per instructions of the Atomic Army, so that they did not fall into the hands of the S.A.S.

"I have just heard some interesting news on the T.V.," said Taff One.

"What is it?" asked Leader.

"The English Government has changed the name of our first objective from Windscale to Sellafield."

"Good heavens," said Evans, "what will these fiends do next? Is there no depth that they won't sink to?"

"I think they are trying to confuse the Atomic Army," said Leader.

"Well, I'm confused, for one," said Evans. "Why do they bother? They must realise that we in the Atomic Army have a high I.Q. level."

"There he goes again," said Taff One, "assuming that I know what an I.Q. is. I Q for bread; I Q for tickets; could the S.A.S. know all about this? If they do, then they must have a spy satellite, but with this weather they could never track the Atomic Army with certainty."

"Perhaps they are doing it with hang-gliders," said Taff One.

"That would account for the big birds that have been following us for the past two weeks," said Leader.

"The quicker we can go on leave, the better it will be for the Atomic Army," said Evans. "They can't possibly glide in three directions at the same time, and they won't know which way Atomic headquarters is."

"We had better go our different ways as soon as the next meal is over," said Leader.

"How do you intend to travel on your leave, Leader?" asked Taff One.

"Oh, I think I shall travel by public transport, to avoid any undue suspicion," said Leader.

"Where do you intend to go?" asked Evans.

"I'll send you a postcard after I get there," said Leader.

"Well, that at least will be something to look forward to; I do like to receive things in the mail," said Evans.

"Didn't Aunty Flo write to you when we were on the canal?" asked Leader.

"Yes, she did," replied Evans, "but that seems ages ago now."

"What I would like to know is how did she know where to write to," said Leader.

"Well, I must admit that Aunty Flo has a very nice hobby," said Evans.

"And what is that?" asked Leader.

"She collects postcards and sticks them in an album," said Evans. She is noted for her collection, and she gives talks in the *Merched y Wawr*."

"And what is that to do with us?" asked Leader.

"It has nothing to do with us as such," replied Evans. "*Merched y Wawr* is the Welsh equivalent of the Women's Institute. I have been sending postcards, to enlarge her collection, to add some interest to her talks."

"That means that the S.A.S. have infiltrated your Aunty Flo's club," said Leader.

"More important still is that one of the infiltrators has learned to speak the ancient Welsh tongue," said Taff One.

"Yes, that is indeed a great worry," said Leader. "I think I will have to inform Atomic One headquarters, so that they can give us fresh orders."

"That will be the best idea," said Taff One, who was just wishing to make his contribution to the discussion.

Another meal vanished almost as fast as it was served up.

"That's much better, now we can really go on leave," said Leader.

Evans was the first to start, and before very long he appeared as a hopping dot on the horizon.

"I'm sure I could write a poem to his movements," said Taff One.

"Why don't you do just that? Then, perhaps, we could enter it for the Eisteddfod, when we go there," said Leader.

A bus came along, and Leader bade farewell to Taff One, jumped aboard and disappeared down the gangway. Taff One was now alone at long last, and he put his Plan B into operation - he would stay here for his three weeks leave, and that would save him having to travel, as that had always made him feel pooped. Anyway, someone had to be here to welcome back the Atomic Army, when it reformed.

"In the meantime, I will have to start on my poem, if I'm to win a prize at the Eisteddfod," thought Taff One. "First of all, I will need a pen and some paper - now where did I see them? I know, they are with the maps in the sidecar of the tandem."

And with that, he hopped to the sidecar as fast as he could. "Ah, here they are," he exclaimed. "Now for some really deep thinking."

He wrote a number of subject headings and sat back to wait for the muses to strike, but before he could think of the first word, he closed his eyes and took a quick forty winks. He woke up to find that it was now night-time, and the sun had gone for the day. He picked up his pen and paper, and moved under a street lamp, where he started to write:

Haunting eyes search the soul,
Trembling fingers clutch the night.
The Darkness is always cold.
Warmth will come with the light.

"Not bad for my first attempt," he thought. "I'll have another go tomorrow." That night he slept in the comfort of the tandem, and was surprised that there was so much room. In the morning, after a late breakfast, he again picked up his pencil and paper and started to write:

Bumble bees, like helicopters
Looking for a landing pad.
Little fish are caught by herons.
Some things are awfully sad.
Voles scurry in the hedgerows,
Moles are blinking in the light.
Caterpillars eating, crawling,
Froglets jumping out of sight.

"I think that might be even better than the first one," thought Taff One.

Three more days passed by, and not a word from Leader or Evans. "So, they must be enjoying themselves," thought Taff One. It rained for the next two days, so there were now only two weeks left before the big push south. The seventh day was a real scorcher, and Taff One spent most of it just admiring nature, when all of a sudden the muse struck him again. With his pencil and paper placed on a flat rock, he suddenly started to write his third poem. "If I keep on at this rate, I will have to have a second opinion as to which one to enter in the competition." He wrote:

Honey bees revving up,
Nectar in a petal cup,
Little heads popping in,
Pollen stuck upon the chin.
Country sounds in the air,
Sunshine glinting on the trees,
Apple blossom hanging down,
Sunbathing lizards on a stone,
Everything is fresh and clean,
As ducks forage by the stream.

"I think I'll sign that with my *nom de plume*," he thought. Then, with no more ado, he signed it 'Taff Two'. He spent an uneasy night, and had difficulty getting to sleep. When he awoke, his next poem plopped into his head, and he searched for his pencil and paper, and he wrote:

The last rabbit says good night,
Goes down his burrow for the night.
Fleeting glance of the hunter's moon,
As dark clouds float across the sky.
Will the morning come too soon,
Or is this our last goodbye? signed Taff Two.

"Oh, dear, I hope that this last line is just a line and not a prediction, because some of my family are psychic."

The postman called at the tandem next day and delivered a postcard from Gretna Green. It showed a view of the old Smithy and the anvil where couples used to be married, and it was signed 'Leader'.

"Well, I never," exclaimed Taff One. "Fancy him going all the way up there on his own. I only hope he knows the way back." Another two days passed, and then another postcard from Leader arrived. This time he was in the Trossachs, and his card had a beautiful view of the lochs and the steamer which took visitors for a cruise.

"I hope he isn't spending all the Atomic Army Funds," Taff

One thought. Next day came a card from Evans, from Blaenau Ffestiniog - a picture of a train that went into the underground workings. He said that the weather was fine and sunny. "I wouldn't have thought you needed it fine and sunny, if you were underground," mused Taff One, "but, there we are." There was a P.S. on the card. "I think I will return a week early - signed Evans"

"Wait a minute," said Taff One to himself, "the postmark says Florence, and the stamp is Italian. Could this be another decoy to confuse the S.A.S., I wonder. I had better send a postcard as well, so the other two don't suspect that I didn't go anywhere."

Another week passed without another poem being written, and Taff One thought that the muse must have taken a holiday as well. Evans arrived back in camp, with a beautiful fur tan and a passionate liking for pasta.

"How did you enjoy your holiday in Blaenau Ffestiniog?" asked Taff One.

"Well, to tell you the truth, I didn't go there," said Evans. "I went on a package tour to Italy."

"Florence, was it?" asked Taff One.

"Yes, it was, wasn't it," agreed Evans. "I wanted to see the art galleries and the sculptures in that city. It would also confuse the S.A.S., should they be checking the mail."

"What did you manage to see?" asked Taff One.

"Well, I did go to see the Uffizi Art Gallery, to see Botticelli's *The Birth of Venus*, and it was very impressive, but the highlight of my stay was my visit to the Academia, to see Michael Angelo's sculpture called *The David*. Where did you go, Taff One?" asked Evans.

I must admit that I haven't left this location, but I haven't been bored. I have been writing poems to enter in the Eisteddfod."

"What a good idea. Perhaps I could write one, and then we could have two entries in the Eisteddfod," said Evans.

"Splendid. Here's some paper and a pencil - off you go."

Evans went off into a quiet corner and was seen scratching his head and mumbling to himself. Finally, after about two hours, he produced his poem entitled:

The David

Sixteen feet of living stone,
Hewn by an artist who was known
And in his lifetime did achieve
The immortality to dream.

"That should do it," said Evans.

"I quite like it, too," said Taff One. "Perhaps, when Leader arrives back, he could have a go at one; he's always maintained that there are prize winning poets in his family."

"But it might only be him saying that to impress us," said Evans.

The following days were warm and sunny, and the two members of the Atomic Army took full advantage of this unusual weather, for this location and for this time of year, to spend the time sunbathing and brewing the dandelion leaves, which were readily at hand. The day for the return of Leader arrived and passed without any sign of him. Evans and Taff One did have a talk about it, and decided to wait until next day before calling a meeting of Atomic One. Next day came and went, and still there was no sign of Leader.

Chapter Six

"We shall have to post him AWOL."

"What exactly does that mean, Evans, in Rabbit language, that is?"

"That should be pretty obvious. It means Atomic Wabbit Off Location, and it's quite a serious offence, one that might attract a fine of six carrots," explained Evans.

A taxi stopped by the tandem, and who should pop out, carrying two large parcels, but Leader.

"Hello, fellow members of the Atomic Army. It is I, laden down with presents and other goodies for your delight," said Leader. Taff One and Evans showed their obvious delight by letting their ears drop to shoulder level.

"First, to undo the blue parcel." He pulled at the string, and out fell a tartan octopus.

"This is for you, Evans, to practice all the ancient melodies which have been buzzing around in your head. I think you blow down this bit here, to puff up the bag there, and then you try and stop the air escaping through those holes by there."

"It seems very complicated to me," said Evans, "but I'll have a go. Thank you very much for thinking about me. I'm very touched."

And now came the red parcel for Taff One. Whatever could it be? He pulled at the string and, lo and behold, a selection of miniature jams and marmalades, a stuffed pouch containing meat and vegetables, which Leader called a haggis, and a lettuce which, frankly, had seen better days.

"These are for you, Taff One. There is also a book of Robert Burns's poems, which I thought might help you to write a poem for the Eisteddfod."

"I've already written four, and Evans has written one, so you see, we are quite prepared for the competition," said Taff One.

"We were hoping that, as Leader, you could manage to come up with something suitable," said Evans.

"You had better leave me alone to think," said Leader.

He climbed into the tandem, pulled the cover up to keep out the draught, and put his paper on a stiff piece of card he had found on the floor. He tapped his pencil, then sucked the end, then he chewed it a bit, before the actual words came to mind. Then he started to write:

As Leader of this Atomic Band
Heading for the promised land,
We can but try and reach our goal
And get retrained at Wookey Hole.
You made me Leader, so you see
The brightest star of we three
Will lead you safely and with class
Through woods and glades and long grass.
Avoiding danger as we go,
Be it S.A.S., rain or snow,
To reach headquarters and to meet
Chief Atomic One, who has big feet.

"Well, that's my offering for now," said Leader, after reading it out loud. The others applauded and shouted 'Bravo!' Leader thanked them for their encouragement, and suggested that they all have an early night. They all put on their nightclothes, but Leader had a tartan night cap, which seemed to add a bit of class to this non-event. Evans wanted to pipe the last post on his tartan Octopus, but Taff One managed to persuade him not to.

Leader was the first to wake. He folded his night cap and put it carefully away in the bottom of the tandem. "I think I will write another poem before breakfast," he thought, and he started to write:

Melons you cannot see
Hanging down from a tree.
This, of course, is profound,
As melons grow upon the ground.
Butterflies don't fly at night,
Because they haven't got a light.
Moths will do so, pretty soon,
Because they know about the moon.
Spiders' webs pearled with dew,
Bluebottles that fly straight through,
Making holes in the net,
Mend it now - catch one yet.
Elves, goblins and fairy rings,
Very strange and eerie things,
Dark black bats that cross the moon,
I hope this poem's ending soon.

Evans stretched and said, "Good Morning." Taff One started yawning, but was the first to rise.

"I'll have tea and toast with marmalade, if there is any going," he said.

"I think it's Evans's turn to make the breakfast," said Leader.

"Are you sure about that? I seem to recall making the last one before we took our leave," said Evans.

"As Leader, I feel I must issue a direct order: Taff One, you make it."

"I don't mind. At least, I can have lashings of marmalade," said Taff One.

"After breakfast, we had better call a meeting of Atomic

One," said Leader.

With breakfast over, Atomic One reconvened and all members were present.

"First on the agenda is the purchase of three tickets for our trip to the International Eisteddfod in Llangollen."

"I vote we do that," said Taff One.

"I second that," said Evans.

"Motion carried," said Leader.

Next on the agenda was the sale of the portable television.

"I vote that we sell, " said Evans.

"I second that," said Taff One.

"T.V. carried down to the second-hand shop," said Leader. "Any other business?" There was no reply, and the meeting closed. Leader sold the portable T.V. Evans was sent down the road to purchase the three tickets, which he duly did. The trip was due to start at 7.30 am, on the following day, and he hopped back to inform the others of this fact.

Next morning arrived and all were awake early and quite excited at the prospect of a nice ride in a bus, a high class bus, of course. They pushed the tandem to the picking-up point, and persuaded the driver to make room for it in the otherwise empty boot. They got on the bus - Taff One first, then Evans followed by Leader. All sat at the rear of the bus and blended in with the locals.

The bus driver waited for the bus to fill up, and checked the members of the public against a list he had from head office. Then, up popped a traffic warden, who threatened to book him if he didn't get off the double yellow lines. The driver muttered a few sharp sentences like, "Why don't you go and help the government? I'm sure that your help would be much sought after." He started the engine, rang the bell twice and off they went.

The first three sets of traffic lights were against them, which did nothing for his peace of mind. This culminated in a bit of speed along a straight bit of road. Unfortunately, the speed was in excess of the speed limit, and the inevitable happened - a radar trap hidden in a lay-by, and a man in a blue helmet flashing the bus to slow down.

"Ah," thought Leader,

"The radar trap is made by man,
A trap to catch us, and they can,
And they do, and they did.
There goes a few more quid.

"Oh, I must write that down as my third poem."

Details were taken by the man in the blue helmet, and the driver wished him a nice day, and off they went again. It was a pleasant journey, with a stop at the English-Welsh border for refreshments. There were no border guards, which Leader viewed with suspicion, and no officials boarded the bus to check passports. Could an attack by the S.A.S. be imminent?

They all returned to their seats and, ding, ding, off they went for the last part of the journey to Llangollen. There were no more hold-ups and all agreed it had been an opal type of a day. The tandem was unloaded from the boot and pushed to a cycle shop for immediate, essential repairs. This was duly done, by a man who was accustomed to mending leaks of all sorts. He was known locally as Taffy Tyres, he wore a peaked cap with the button undone and a pair of glasses with lenses like milk bottle bottoms. They asked him how much for the total job.

"To tell you the truth," he said, "you're the first customers I've had since decimalisation; that's what made me give it up, you see. I just couldn't get used to the new ways."

"Well, would four pounds cover it?" asked Leader.

"I think that would be quite fair," replied Taffy Tyres.

They paid him, and he invited them over to the local hostelry, where he ordered a drink all round. It was only a stroke of luck that there were only four present, otherwise they would have finished the four pounds in the first round.

The afternoon was spent in looking at the different parties, who were performing their different types of musical acts, and then there was the dancing, in the different national costumes, that made a blaze of colour on the Eisteddfod field.

"With all these attractive females about, let's hold a beauty and deportment contest," said Taff One.

"We had better offer a good prize for the winner, and quite an attractive one for the runner-up," said Leader.

"What can we offer?" asked Evans. "After all, we don't have a bottomless money bag."

"I know. Let's offer the Queendom of the Atomic Army, and the runner-up can have the title of Princess of the Atomic Army."

"That's a splendid idea, Taff One," said Leader.

Posters were prepared and hung. Twenty contestants entered, and these were whittled down to seven; some of those that fell by the wayside had things like speech impediments, tufts of fluff missing, broken whiskers, and one unfortunate had an elastic stocking and a bandaged foot, but the seven that remained appeared to be in one piece.

Another selection was made, with the contestants modelling crash helmets, sun glasses and wellingtons, until only two remained: Flora Skimpossidi, a rather thin Belgian, and Pamela Plump, who was a little on the round side and came from Plympton, wherever that might be. The decision was left in the capable hands of the three Atomic Judges, who were left in quite a dilemma. Tubby or not tubby; that was the question.

"I vote for Flora," said Leader.

"And I vote for Pamela," said Evans.

"That, I suppose, leaves it down to me," said Taff One.

"Well, what have you decided?" asked Leader.

"I'm not sure," said Taff One.

"Well, you'd better hurry up. I think they are nodding off," said Evans.

There was a twitching of tails and a wringing of paws as Taff One rose to give the final verdict. He spoke:

"I will give the result in reverse order. In second place, and Princess of the Atomic Army, your judges have put Pamela. And the winner of this, the first contest, and winner of the Queendom of the Atomic Army, your judges have voted Stella von Spinnach."

There was a scream of delight from the rear of the stage as Stella tripped forward, in her elastic stocking and bandaged foot, to take the title. Flora, in the meantime, threw a wobbly and flaked out. She fell into the official throne and got jammed there, and no matter how they tried, they were unable to move her. She was heard to mutter, "Fix; unfair; she must be a relative of the judges; boo-boo-boo; I demand a recount; send for the organisers; I'll tell my mother."

In fact, Flora was not very happy with the result at all. She did brighten up somewhat when the crown didn't fit and slid down over Stella's eyes and perched on her nose. Leader was the first to speak.

"We can't have Stella as Queendom of the Atomic Army; she was eliminated in the first selection. How did Taff One come out with Stella?"

"I've always had a soft spot for those who are in pain, or are otherwise disadvantaged," said Taff One.

"A very honourable sentiment, but hardly conducive to the occasion, I would have thought," said Evans.

"Good grief! Where did he get all those big words from?" thought Taff One.

"We had better have a meeting of the judges," said Leader.

"Now, come on, all these people are waiting to see fair play," said Evans.

"Well, you had better break the news to Stella, Taff One," said Leader.

"How am I to do that without hurting her feelings?"

"That's up to you, but you had better think of something quickly; I think it goes dark in five hours time," said Leader.

"I know, we'll appoint her as third in line to the Queendom, and as such we will give her the freedom of the parish," said Taff One.

"Phew! I think you might have solved a very tricky problem. Go and tell her," said Leader.

"Excuse me, Miss Stella, but could I have a word," said Taff One.

"Of course you can, young man, but it's Mrs. Stella von Spinnach," said Stella.

"I'm afraid there has been a very unfortunate error: due to the rule book, you have to be an unmarried lady to enter the competition. I hope you understand. It's very unfortunate, but there we are, rules are rules."

"Oh, I understand. It was very kind of you to pick me, even if it was an error," said Stella.

"Taff One reported all this to the two others, who thanked him for his efforts. The three spent a very pleasant time in Llangollen, and by the end of the week they were full up, from their tails to their ears, in nice folk culture. They had stayed in a bed and breakfast cottage, with a man who claimed to be an undercover hermit. He was a member of every club in the district, and that, he said, was the clever bit about being undercover.

Next on the list was to locate the direction of Offa's Dyke, and to proceed to get there with haste, avoiding capture by the S.A.S.

"I know," said Evans, "let's go for another trip on the canal."

"What for? You seem obsessed by water," said Leader.

"Pity he doesn't use more of it to wash behind his ears," thought Taff One.

"We haven't anything better to do this afternoon, so why not have a nice trip on the water?" asked Evans.

"Let's put it to the vote," said Leader. All three voted in favour, so the motion was carried, and off they went, in the direction of the canal, riding the tandem, which was now in working order, and even the bell rang.

They boarded the barge and put the tandem in the prow. The scenery was spectacular, and when they crossed the aqueduct, Evans had difficulty sitting down, and he had greater difficulty in clutching the parachute and putting it on.

"What happens if this lot gets a leak?" wondered Evans. "I suppose they send for a sky plumber, but where he finds the stop tap is anybody's guess."

There was no leak, so the journey sailed on unhindered.

"I think we have committed an error of judgement," said Leader.

"And, pray, what have we failed to do this time?" asked Evans.

"Well, remember when we arrived at the Welsh-English border - we must have passed Offa's Dyke," said Leader.

"Well, all is not lost. All we have to do is make our way back to the border and we've cracked it," said Taff One.

"Where's the compass and the map? Let's get it right this time," said Leader.

"Evans took a reading and made a mark on the map. The tandem was stocked with goodies, and the Atomic Army mounted it and moved towards the border. It was getting dusk when they spotted a small canal with an ancient limekiln built under the side of the bank.

"We'll camp here for the night, as it seems quite secure," said Leader. "I remember staying in one of these things before, when we had a downpour. I vote we put our tent up in that field over there, at least we'll have a chance to escape in all directions, and not be trapped by the canal wall, should we be attacked."

But, what had happened to the tent? No matter where they looked, it could not be found.

"It looks as if that idea has taken a nose-dive," said Leader.

"What do we do now?" asked Evans.

"Let's hire a caravan for the weekend," said Taff One.

"Where do we get one of those from? I haven't seen one for hire in the last ten miles," said Evans.

"That's it then; it's into the ancient limekiln," said Leader.

"I don't want to do that, as it makes my ears pop," said Taff One.

"I think you could cure that if you took your balaclava off," said Evans.

"Do you really think so, Evans? If so, I'll give it a try." And with that, he pulled the balaclava off, to reveal a big curler in his hair.

"Whatever is that for?" asked Leader.

"I wanted to look presentable when I went to collect the poetry prize," said Taff One.

"I knew there was something in the back of my mind," said Leader.

"What was that?" asked Evans.

"We forgot to enter the poems for the judges to consider," said Leader. "Great, great, great. We burst our butt composing poems, which are then completely forgotten about. However will we become famous in the art world, if we are overlooked by ourselves, never mind the public! Well, never mind, let's make ourselves comfortable tonight, for a good early start in the morning. Offa's Dyke, here we come."

They all settled down for the night, but nobody could get to sleep.

"I know," said Evans. "Let's hold a poetry competition."

"But, we've already written poems for the Eisteddfod."

"Those cannot be included in this present competition," said Leader. "We all make a line, each in turn, until we have a three verse poem. I'll start."

"The wombat flies like a bird," - you go next, Taff One.

"And sings songs you've never heard," - now your go, Evans.

"They cannot nest in trees,

Because they have wobbly knees."

"Well, that will have to do for the first verse. Now you've got the idea, we'll pick a subject and have a go from there. How about a poem on canals and canal banks?"

"I'll start it off this time," said Taff One, "and we'll compose a verse each."

"Dragonflies that dart and hover,
Land on water with no bother.
Lurex wings that flap and glimmer,
Casting shadows in sun's shimmer"

"Now you, Evans."

"Bulrushes with fluffy tops, yet
Bending with the breezes.
Frogs and toads are always wet,
But you never hear their sneezes."

"Now, my go," said Leader.

"Water boatmen sliding by,
No sound, not a whisper,
Still they stamp their feet to try
To make the water blister."

"Well, I think we've had enough of that for one evening. Let's make a concerted effort to nod off until morning."

Dawn broke, breakfast was eaten, the tandem packed and mounted, a compass bearing taken, the map read.

"Tally ho, off to go," said Leader.

They reached a sign that read, "OFFA'S DYKE", and an arrow pointed the way.

"Well, we are on course this time," said Evans. "I knew this compass would come in handy."

Another stroke of bad luck - someone had turned the sign to point in the wrong direction, and the intrepid three cycled into a farmyard. All of a sudden the three were surrounded by geese.

"I don't like geese," said Leader, "not even for Christmas dinner."

"I wouldn't invite any of these home for Christmas," said Evans.

"It's ganders I don't like," said Taff One. "They are always bad tempered and peck you without provocation."

"Well, at least we know that the Atomic Army don't like geese," said Leader.

"What do you suggest we do now?" asked Evans.

"How about doing an about turn and pedalling like mad?" said Taff One.

"That seems to fit the bill and that's what we'll do," said Leader.

They turned the tandem around and started to pedal like mad and, as they passed the gander, on their way out, he pecked the side of the tandem and made a sound like a machine gun.

"I'm sure he must have been trained by the S.A.S." said Leader.

"I thought we'd given them the slip," said Evans.

"So did I," said Taff One.

"Better pedal a bit harder, then," said Leader.

They made it out of the yard and back down the lane, and headed for the signpost.

"Ah, there it is. Now all we have to do is work out which way that arrow should have been pointing," said Leader.

Evans once again took out his compass and took a reading.

"Have you got it right this time?" asked Taff One.

"Of course I have," replied Evans.

"Let me have a look at your compass," said Leader.

"Certainly. Here it is," said Evans.

"I thought so. This is a barometer, for forecasting weather, and not a compass," said Leader.

"Are you absolutely sure about that? They told me at that night school that it was a compass," said Evans.

"Well, you look here," said Leader. "It predicts that it will be fine tomorrow."

"Well, that's something to look forward to," said Taff One.

"Never mind that," said Evans. "I'm going to write that night school a stiff letter, when I get hold of a piece of cardboard."

"I don't think it will do any good, but you can but try," said Leader.

"They might give me a refund of the fees I paid," said Evans.

"Some hope of that, but we'll have a go at them anyway," said Leader.

"Let's take that path over there, the one with the acorn sign on it. I think that's a sign put down by a government department to classify a footpath," said Taff One.

They pushed the tandem along the narrow path for about two miles; when they came to a bend in the path, they went around the bend and arrived at a gate leading into a field, and there, in the middle, was an oak tree.

"So much for government departments, Taff One," rebuked Leader.

"Oak trees must be pretty scarce around here, to have their very own sign."

"Not to worry. We'll do an about turn again, and this time we will take the correct route, as there is only one way left to go from that signpost," said Leader.

Back they went to the signpost, and this time they arrived just in time to see the council taking it away.

"Excuse me, sir," said Taff One," but why are you removing that signpost?"

"It's council policy. All signs must now be bilingual, so we are bringing a fresh one tomorrow," said the council foreperson. And off they went.

"I'm starving," said Evans.

"Me, too," said Leader.

"What are we going to have?" asked Taff One.

"I fancy wild yarrow," said Evans.

"I think it's still in season, although I don't recall having seen any," said Leader.

"I fancy a nice, fresh lettuce," said Taff One.

"Don't we all," said Evans, "but I think we'll have to settle for turnip tops, there seems to be a field full planted over there."

The Atomic Three gorged themselves on the turnip tops until they could eat no more. An Atomic snooze session was called for, and voted for by a unanimous show of paws.

"Do we really have to wait until those council chaps replace the sign before we can proceed any further?" asked Evans.

"Yes, we do," said Leader, "or they might think it odd that we went, not knowing the correct direction, and report the matter back. That's how the S.A.S. get their information, and we could be captured in an eye blink."

"I think you mean in the wink of an eye, Leader," said Taff One.

"Never mind that. Let's kip down here until they come back," said Leader.

PRIVATE - KEEP OUT - SECRET WELSH ATOMIC RABBIT
ARMY MEETING
THIS WAY
ATOMIC ONE
LEADER
MEETING IN PROGRESS

TAFF ONE

Chapter Seven

It was a very heavy snooze that the three Atomic Army members had, and they only woke up because Leader's tummy was rumbling like a glass marble falling over a corrugated sheet. The council workers arrived back, and unloaded their picks and shovels and post hole borer. The foreperson blew his whistle, and they all jumped into action and leaned on their shovels. Two, who didn't have any tools, leaned against each other. It looked a bit like rain, so it was decided to have a brew-up. This was done, and they all sat around and chatted, drank their tea and pointed in the direction of the job that was waiting to be done. The foreperson blew his whistle and everyone jumped to their feet, made their way over to the job site and peered down the old hole that the old signpost had come from.

"Can't we use the same hole?" asked one of the men. "Then we won't have to use the post hole borer. Fred's on holiday, so there's nobody here who can operate it, anyway."

"We'll use the original hole, then. Better make it a little larger, so that the new signpost fits in snugly." This they did.

"Right," said the foreperson, "get the new sign from the lorry; that is, of course, if one of you remembered to load it at the depot."

Two of the men went to the lorry and collected the sign.

"Shouldn't we get a well-known dignitary to do the honours by planting the new sign in the hole?"

"Let's ask the local mayor," said Taff One.

"I don't think that's flashy enough. How about asking royalty?" suggested Evans.

"You know what month it is; they'll all be up in Scotland, at their house up there," said Leader.

"Well, that smacks another good idea in the designer bucket," said Taff One.

"I know, let's ask the foreperson's wife to do the honours," said Evans.

"That's a good idea," said Leader. "Go and ask him."

"Excuse me, Mr. Foreperson, but would your wife be willing to be the dignitary to put the signpost in the hole," said Taff One.

"I don't know if she can manage that with all her other duties," said the foreperson.

"What other duties does she have?" asked Leader.

"Well, she's a lollipop lady, and after that she helps with the school dinners; then, today being Wednesday, she goes to her bingo club. She's been quite lucky lately; she's won a week's holiday in Italy for two, a plastic bucket and spade and a computerised knitting machine, but I'll ask her anyway."

With that, he took an extended lunch hour and arrived back hand-in-hand with his lady wife.

The signpost was slipped into the hole, and the foreperson's wife said, "I declare this footpath open. God bless her and all that walk on her."

The Atomic Army applauded and were joined by the council workmen. In fact, everybody had a very happy afternoon, especially when the council workmen produced a pot of hot tea and some jam sandwiches.

After this unexpected buffet, Leader decided that the time was ripe for the Atomic Army to make their way to Offa's Dyke, before someone else moved it. Off they went, after bidding the council workmen goodbye. They travelled about a mile before discovering that the tandem was still at the signpost.

"Oh, bother. You go and get it, Taff One," said Leader.

"Why does it have to be me every time something goes wrong," said Taff One.

"I'm Leader, and you obey orders, that's why! So, off you go."

Half an hour passed, and Taff One arrived with the tandem, his face red with the effort, and he was puffing a bit after the unexpected pedalling.

"You may rest before we go on," said Leader.

Ten minutes passed, and Taff One recovered his composure, so Leader thought it was now convenient to proceed to Offa's Dyke. They went on for another mile, and passed a couple of field mice, who were eating ripe blackberries in the hedgerow.

"Nice day," said one mouse, "care to join us? I think there's plenty for everyone."

"No thank you. We must press on to Offa's Dyke before nightfall," said Leader.

"Well, you haven't very far to go before you reach it," said the second mouse, who, by this time, had managed to cover his face with blackberry juice, and looked very much like a black and white minstrel.

The Atomic Three carried on and, lo and behold, they came to another signpost, with *CLAWDD OFFA* and *OFFA'S DYKE* on it, with an arrow pointing in the direction they had just come from.

"Well, look at that," said Evans. "I wonder who planted that one."

"Well, it wasn't me," said Taff One.

"We know that," said Leader.

"Where did we go wrong this time?" said Evans.

"If I knew that, we wouldn't have got it wrong," said Leader.

"Let's back track to those two mice we saw and enquire

again," said Evans.

"Good idea," said Taff One.

Back the Atomic Army went. The two mice were asleep in the hedgerow.

"Squeak ho! You two, squeak ho! I'm so sorry to disturb you, but could you re-direct us three to that elusive Offa's Dyke?"

"Certainly. Go back to the signpost which says *CLAWDD OFFA - OFFA'S DYKE* and the arrow which points back this way, turn the post around through ninety degrees, then follow the arrow for three hundred yards, and there it is," said the first mouse.

"We'll do just that. Thanks a bunch," said Leader.

Back they went to the signpost, turned it through ninety degrees, and followed the arrow for three hundred yards to a high, green bank.

"This must be it," said Evans, "although it doesn't look much like a dyke to me. Where's the water?"

"You really are obsessed by water, Evans," said Leader.

"Why do they call it a dyke, then?" asked Evans.

"It's a dry dyke, because if there had been water, it would have run down the wall and filled Wookey Hole and ruined our retraining area," said Leader.

"Well, that explains that," said Taff One. "Let's make camp here, as night is beginning to fall. It will probably be quite dark in an hour."

"Better try and rustle up some grub, then," said Evans.

"Nothing fancy for me," said Leader.

Taff One went away on a food search, and returned with a box full of dock leaves and bramble tips, and a hint of sorrel for taste. They had their meal and made a snug nest in the long grass, parked the tandem nearby and all piled in the nest for the night.

"I think I'll clean my boots," said Evans. "There may be an

inspection in the morning."

After he had finished the boots, it was now quite dark; a voice was heard to say, "How do you know that it's your boots you've cleaned?"

"Oh, dear. I'll have to clean all of them now, to make sure that I have," said Evans.

It took him another hour to finish, and he was quite tired when he managed to get his head down for the night. But at least they had reached Offa's Dyke and the plan was beginning to take shape.

It was a nice, crisp morning, with the dew lying thickly on the grass. Evans started to do some exercises, to get rid of the stiffness that he felt. Taff One scurried about looking for tasty titbits for breakfast. All he could find at first were vinegar leaves, but then a stroke of good fortune - a greengrocer's cart passed. It hit a bump, which dislodged a crate containing lettuce onto the path. He tried in vain to attract the attention of the greengrocer, but said, "Waste not, want not," picked up the crate and took it back to camp.

"I see you've had a vegi-gram," said Leader.

"I did try and attract the greengrocer's attention, but I don't think he could understand Wabbit."

The lettuce tasted as sweet as they could wish, and after clearing away the breakfast, loading the tandem, and the Atomic Army had been inspected, they were at last ready to resume the push south.

"Hoppi ho, here we go," said Leader.

"I do wish he would stop using those stupid sayings," thought Evans.

They travelled another four miles, but had to stop because some of the dyke had been removed, leaving a big gap, which had to be skirted around. The Atomic Three tried to lift the tandem down the bank, and up the bank on the other side, but it turned out to be too heavy.

"I think we'll have to unload the tandem, to make it a lot lighter," said Leader.

They started to unload underwater wet suits, flippers, maps, string, a safety pin, the first aid box, a barometer, which Evans insisted was a compass, one gent's long-tailed jacket, a bowler hat, a tartan octopus, two small pots of jam and a box of shortcake biscuits. After seeing all these unloaded and placed in a pile, Leader was heard to remark, "No wonder the tent went missing. There was no room for it, anyway."

They could now safely lift the tandem down the slope, and by playing an old Christmas game called Pass-the-Parcel, they were able to get the contents down as well. The next bit proved to be more difficult - getting back up the slope with the tandem.

"I suggest we leave it here and go on foot. I'm sure we could make more headway," said Taff One.

"What a stupid way to think of improving our lot - by getting rid of our main asset. Where did you receive your education?" questioned Leader.

"We'll have to borrow a length of rope and, by a clever system of pulleys, we will overcome this small difficulty," said Evans.

"Well, that's got the theory over with; now for the practical. But, where do we get some rope?" said Leader.

"There's a farm over there. Try and borrow some rope from there, Evans."

"I don't like farms," said Evans. "They always have dangerous things hanging about, to either pounce on you, fall on you, or for you to fall in."

"Nevertheless, you'll have to go," said Leader.

"I'll go, but under protest," said Evans. "If I'm not back in an hour, send a search party."

Evans came back in twenty minutes, looking like a jumble sale item, his hair in disarray, one ear bent and tufts of fur missing, but with a length of half inch hessian over his shoulder.

"I see you managed it, then," said Leader, "but do try and

tidy yourself up. You look an absolute mess."

"Thank you so much for the vote of thanks," said Evans.

"What happened to you?" asked Taff One. "Not more geese, I hope."

"No, not this time. I met an over friendly billy goat, who insisted we play Butt-the-Intruder. I agreed, only to find out too late that the Intruder was me," said Evans.

"You poor thing, you must have been quite concerned for your safety," said Taff One.

"That, if I may say so, is the understatement of the year."

"Never mind all that now, pass me the rope," said Leader.

The rope was duly tied to the tandem, and with two pulling at the top of the slope, and Leader steering from the bottom, the tandem was duly persuaded to the top once more.

"Don't forget to load the stores," said Leader, who disappeared behind a clump of gorse, and left it to the other two to do the trivial jobs.

The Atomic Three again boarded the tandem, with Leader, sitting in the sidecar giving directions.

"I don't think he knows how to pedal," thought Evans.

"Idle so and so," thought Taff One, "he could do with some exercise; he's developing quite a tummy; where he used to hop, hop, hop, he now hop, wobble, hop, wobble, hops."

They pedalled and pedalled and the miles seemed to drift away. The Atomic Three were again getting hungry and, yet again, Offa's Dyke had come to an abrupt end.

"Out with the rope again," said Leader. There was another repeat performance, then the hunt was on for eaties: blackberries, dock leaves and half a dozen acorns and some wild mushrooms, not a lot of any, but just enough of each to make quite a delicate meal. They washed it down with dandelion milk. Leader always did have a nice touch when it came to the culinary arts.

Back on the tandem again, they travelled a few more

miles with nothing much happening, except for a few clouds that scurried by, and those were up quite high. The Atomic Three encountered some more gaps in the dyke, and it was decided to call a meeting of Atomic One. All members were again present.

"I propose that we abandon our trek south via Offa's Dyke," said Evans. "All we seem to be doing is lugging the tandem up and down like a yo-yo."

"What's a yo-yo?" asked Taff One.

"It's like a piece of oval wood wound around with string. It goes up and down, unwinding itself, and then winding itself up again," said Leader.

"That's all very well, but why is it called a yo-yo?" asked Taff One.

"I don't know why," said Leader.

"Neither do I," said Evans, "but it is."

"Well, that's all very enlightening; thanks for the explanation," said Taff One, who remained as confused as ever he was.

"I second Evans's proposal," said Leader.

"I third it," said Taff One.

"Motion carried," said Evans.

"What to do next then is the vexing problem," said Leader.

"Well, you're Leader, you suggest something," said Taff One.

"I propose we sleep on the problem until morning; everything is much clearer in the daylight," said Leader.

Another crisp, star-filled night, with shooting stars moving across the sky; the Atomic Three nodded off. The light breeze rustled the leaves, the cry of the owls and the fluttering wings of the bats all added to the noises of the night; moles popped their heads out of hidden tunnels, worms slithered across the grass, and tried to keep out of their way. Even the croak of a frog sounded eerie. All these sounds were going on, but the Atomic Three slept on, proving that what you don't see you don't miss.

The local cockerel cleared his throat, and let fly with the noisy sound that only he could make - dawn had arrived. The Atomic Three awoke, stretched, yawned and shivered.

"What now?" said Evans.

"Yes, what now?" said Taff One.

"Good morning," said Leader. "First things first; I feel like a light breakfast, I don't know about you two."

"How light is light?" thought Evans.

Taff One went off, and returned with a handful of dandelion leaves for everyone.

"Thank you," said Evans, "Is that it?"

"Yes, that's it for now," said Leader.

"Well, as you are all aware, we voted unanimously to get off Offa's Dyke," said Leader.

"I see, it's off the dyke and on the bike," said Taff One. "We should really manage to get a move on now. Well, here we go again"

They pedalled down a straight road and came to a red telephone box.

"Could we stop here for a while?" asked Evans.

"What for now? We were making good headway that time," said Leader.

"I want to 'phone Aunty Flo, it's her birthday, you see, and I've forgotten to send her a card," said Evans.

"Very well, but make it brief," said Leader.

"Can you allow me an advance on my pay?" asked Evans, "preferably in ten pence pieces, for the call, you see."

"Very well, here's four coins, that should do it," said Leader.

Evans went into the box, dialled the number and sang, "*Happy Birthday, Aunty Flo, Happy Birthday to you*". Aunty

Flo said, "Thank you very much, that was very touching. Evans rang off, his halo now back in position.

"Well, that's that," said Leader.

"I think your Aunty Flo's a Leo rabbit, quite a strange combination," said Taff One.

"Remind me to buy a newspaper tomorrow, to check her star forecast."

"There is just one small point: when you are telephoning, there is no need to smile down the telephone, as Aunty Flo can't see you," said Leader.

Back again on the tandem, they went past a sign which said HOPE.

"I knew there was hope, and there it is, to prove it," said Leader.

"We must have come a very long way since we took our last map reading," said Evans.

"From what I can make out on the map, we are just behind that large town called Welshpool, and the road from here is a very straight one, from here to a hill town, with a ruined castle, called Montgomery," said Leader.

"Well, at least, if the road is straight, we can't very well take a wrong turning," said Taff One.

"I'm not keen on turnings, anyway," said Evans.

"We can spend the night in the ruins of the castle; nobody will be there after dark, it will be too spooky," said Leader.

"That's all I need," said Taff One, " a scary place to make my hair stand on end, after brushing it flat."

A quick snack, then the Atomic Three reached the castle ruins, just before nightfall, found a sheltered spot out of the prevailing wind, and camouflaged the tandem. The sheltered spot proved to be a draughty and noisy spot; the wind howled in the broken turrets and rattled the wire fence against the metal posts.

"How are we going to sleep here with all this noise going on," said Evans.

"Well, it's too dark to find another spot, so we'll have to do the best we can here," said Leader.

"It's asking rather a lot, but we'll try to sleep here," said Taff One.

"Good night," said Evans.

"Good night," said Leader.

"I can't sleep," said Taff One. "When I couldn't sleep back home my mother used to read me a story."

"It's too dark to read you a story, so you concentrate on getting your head down," said Leader.

Zzzzz! Zzzzz! Zzzzz!

"There we are, Evans has dropped off already," said Leader, " so come on, sleep, and that's a direct order."

"I could try and put cotton wool in my ears, that sometimes helps," said Taff One.

"Do what you please, but please do it in a hurry," said Leader.

"O.K., but where's the cotton wool?" asked Taff One.

"How am I to know that," said Leader. "It's now dark, and we have camouflaged the tandem too well. I can't remember where we left it."

"I hope you can find it in the morning, I've some jam and biscuits in the sidecar."

Fatigue overtook Leader first, followed a little later by Taff One. They all slept a deep, deep sleep that only fatigued rabbits could sleep. Dawn broke yet again, and the Atomic Three had the first problem of the day: finding the tandem. It proved more difficult than any of the three could imagine.

"You did much too good a job with the camouflage, Evans," said Leader.

"Keep looking, it's bound to be here somewhere," said Evans.

"There it is, over there, and someone has painted it red," said Taff One.

"Oh, dear, the S.A.S. have tumbled us," said Leader.

"Just a second, that over there's a postman's bicycle," said Evans.

"I wonder if he has anything for me," said Taff One.

"Are you expecting anything?" asked Leader.

"No, but it's always nice to have something in the post," said Taff One.

"Keep looking for the tandem, or we will be here another night," said Leader.

"Find it, or find it not, I'm not staying in this draughty ruin another night," said Evans. "It makes my ears go limp."

"Here it is, heavily disguised as a laurel bush," said Taff One.

"Next time I camouflage it, I'll camouflage it as a tandem," said Evans, "then we can find it quicker."

"Come on, you two. Now we've cracked that problem, I think it's about time we had breakfast," said Leader.

A quick rummage in the ruins produced absolutely nothing, and the Atomic Three were forced to go down into the town, to see if there was anything to tickle their palates.

"Look over there," said Evans," a shop that sells organic produce. Have we any cash left in the kitty?"

"We certainly have," said Leader, not telling the other two how much. He hopped over to the shop, opened the door, which triggered off a doorbell's loud Ding! He was in the shop for about ten minutes, and Evans and Taff One were starting to get quite worried, and thought that he'd been captured, but the shop door opened and out staggered Leader, carrying two large carrier bags. He placed the bags in the sidecar, they remounted the tandem and pedalled a mile out of town to a large lay-by, where they dismounted.

"Ah, breakfast at long last," said Evans.

The two carrier bags were lifted out of the tandem.

"Look what I've bought. This will make a pleasant change,

if nothing else," said Leader.

First, he produced a kohlrabi.

"That's an ugly looking swede," said Taff One.

Then he produced a stick of celery.

"I do like to crunch that," said Evans.

"This is all very well, but why didn't you purchase anything to eat?" asked Taff One.

"I did. Have a look in the other carrier," said Leader.

A bunch of fresh, green spinach, some young carrots and some tender french beans were inside.

"That's better. Let's get stuck into this lot," said Evans. "Did you buy anything to drink?"

"Yes, a bottle of Perrier Water," said Leader.

"Your choice of foods is admirable, can we get started. My tummy is crying out for food," said Evans.

The Atomic Three sat down and shared the food between them.

"That was very pleasant, and it was quite cheap to buy," said Leader.

They were again on their way, and a helpful breeze at their backs helped to move them along a bit quicker than just pedalling. They were now approaching Clun, on the way to Knighton.

"I think we will have to travel through Knighton at night," said Leader.

"What will happen when we make our way to Hay-on-Wye?" asked Evans.

"I've heard that they have their own king there," said Taff One.

"That's right, so they might have their own army, and that could be most dangerous for us," said Leader.

Another meeting of Atomic One was called by Leader.

"What's this meeting all about?" asked Evans.

"Well, it's to instill into you the importance of extra vigil, as we are soon to approach the areas around Hereford where the S.A.S. have their headquarters."

"Oh, dear, I knew I was about to worry about something," said Taff One.

"There will be no need to worry, as long as we are prepared for any eventuality," said Leader, "and that is why we must switch our movement to night-time, so we are less conspicuous."

"But, if we travel at night, we shall have to have a light on the tandem, then we will be seen for miles," said Evans.

"I hadn't thought of that," said Leader.

"Better cancel the travelling by night, as we would also have difficulty finding our food," said Taff One.

"That's another thing I hadn't thought of," said Leader.

"Without our food, we would become weak and distressed and would squabble amongst ourselves, and that would never do," said Evans.

The Atomic Three agreed that food was nearly as important as gaining the retraining area at Wookey Hole.

"Remember, we must reach our base in tip-top condition," said Leader. "That's what our Commander-in-Chief expects of us, and that's what our Commander-in-Chief is going to get."

Chapter Eight

"It will be nice to be fit again," said Evans, as he chewed on a piece of celery he'd kept from his last meal.

"Please try not to make that crunching sound in the middle of a meeting of Atomic One, I find it very distracting," said Leader.

"I must apologise for the lax way I have behaved," said Evans.

"We'll let it pass this time, but make sure that it does not occur again," said Leader. "I have no wish to reprimand you in front of Taff One."

"I'm sorry, I did not know it was his turn to be reprimanded," said Evans.

"Shall we get back down to some serious business," said Leader.

"I second that," said Taff One.

"Any other business?" asked Leader.

"Yes, how much money do we have in the kitty?" asked Evans.

Leader gave an embarrassed cough, and pulled out his notebook, where he kept account of the financial details of the Atomic Army.

"It's not right up to date, but to give you an estimate, I think we have somewhere in the region of forty-seven pounds, and that takes into account a contra item of forty pence, which Evans had in lieu of wages, to make that 'phone call to Aunty Flo, to wish her a happy birthday," said Leader.

"Oh, as much as that," said Taff One.

"It's still not enough to hire a taxi to take us to Wookey Hole," said Evans.

"We could not do that, anyway; the rule book states that the Atomic Army must travel incognito and use the cheapest possible means to get about," said Leader.

"What rule book is that?" asked Evans.

"It's the handbook of the Atomic Army, laid down by the All-High Committee of the Atomic Army Welfare Section, 1968," said Leader.

"Good heavens! Hasn't the rule book been updated since then?" asked Evans.

"Time to make another of our famous moves towards our goal," said Taff One.

With the light fading fast, the Atomic Army headed for a wood.

"Remember to avoid small footpaths; that's where the S.A.S. will have laid snares to capture us," said Leader, always vigilant to possible dangers.

"What about food?" asked Taff One.

"It's too dark to find any now," said Leader.

"All that's left is to attack the emergency rations in the tandem," said Taff One.

"There goes my present of jams and biscuits from Scotland," said Evans.

"Never mind, I'll buy replacements when we come to the next shop," said Leader.

The two small jars of jam and the biscuits were removed from the tandem and placed on a piece of white cloth, which had been dyed grey for camouflage purposes. It was with great difficulty that the jams were opened and spread evenly on the biscuits. Leader shared them out.

"One for you, Taff One. Two for you, Evans. Three for me. One for you, Evans. Two for you, Taff One. Three for me. One for me. Two for you, Evans. Three for Taff one. That's it - the end of the packet."

"You shared those out very fairly," said Evans. "The only thing that I cannot understand is how your pile looks bigger than mine."

"Put it down to an optical illusion. You know how close we are to the autumn solstice," said Leader.

"Yes, that must be it. I hadn't thought of that," replied Evans.

They ate the meagre rations, and settled down for the night; this was another eerie affair, with the moon hiding behind clouds, popping out occasionally to make strange shapes of the night. At last, the Atomic Army dropped off, with just the odd slumber being disturbed by the cry of the owls and the scurrying of the voles crunching at snail shells.

A still, sharp dawn broke, and the Atomic Three fell in for inspection. Taff One received a ticking off for having a tuft of fluff missing. Evans was congratulated on a good turn out. Leader avoided inspection.

"That's over. First things first. Now for breakfast," said Evans.

It proved to be difficult to find food in the wood, as the ground was now being covered by the leaves falling from the trees and hiding possible scrummy titbits. There were a few toadstools growing from a rotting tree branch, but as nobody seemed to know if they were poisonous, they took the easy way out and left them where they were.

"I think we'll have to purchase breakfast on this occasion," said Leader.

"Well, let's hurry and try and find a café, I'm starving," said Evans.

All three jumped aboard the tandem, and pedalled for a good hour before they came across a transport café. Dismounting, all three hopped into the café and sat down at the first available table. A waitress in a striped pinny came up with her note pad.

"What will you gents have?" she asked.

"Could we start with three large bowls of porridge," said Leader.

"What else?" she asked, as she started to write the order.

"I'd like a side salad," said Evans.

"Yes, three side salads and a good helping of new potatoes," said Leader. "Oh, and three glasses of milk, please."

"It won't be long. Would you like a newspaper to read while you wait?" she said.

"Yes please. Do you have a copy of *The Rabbit and Stockbreeder*? said Leader.

"Sorry, all we have are the daily papers," she said.

"We'll leave it then," said Leader, as he did not want his two friends to be alarmed by any sensational stories that might be in the dailies.

Breakfast arrived, and was devoured almost as fast as it was put on the table. They asked for the bill, and the total for the three came to seventy-five pence. Leader paid the bill and the three hopped out of the café and made for the tandem.

"Did you leave a tip for the waitress, Leader?" asked Taff One.

"Oh, dear, it completely slipped my mind," said Leader.

"Well, we are not too far from the café, you can still go back," said Evans.

"Do you really think it is necessary; we won't be coming this way again," said Leader.

"I don't think that's the point, and it's rather a selfish attitude to adopt, and it could be construed as rather a cheap move by the Atomic Army," said Evans.

"Yes, you are right. I'll go back and rectify it immediately," said Leader.

He went back to café and gave the waitress a twenty pence tip. She was quite touched, and went back into the kitchen singing. Leader, too, felt better as he went to rejoin his friends.

With hunger satisfied, they remounted the tandem and started to pedal, all, that is, except Leader, who was in the sidecar, about to have a snooze. The sun came out, the sky cleared, birds began to sing and bumblebees began to hum.

"Perhaps, one day they will learn the words, then they could stop all that humming," thought Taff One.

It was going to be a nice day, with a lot of miles covered. Leader missed all the joys of nature, as he had nodded off with the gentle rocking of the tandem and the heat from the sun. He awoke refreshed and asked why the tandem had come to a halt.

"We had to stop, Evans has a nasty corn on his left foot," said Taff One, "and this seat that I'm sitting on is not the most comfortable in the world; I doubt I will be able to hop properly for days."

"It must be time for something to eat," said Leader.

"I'm afraid that you slept through the last meal, Leader," said Evans.

"I don't think that's very fair," said Leader, "letting me sleep on while you two were gorging yourselves."

"Well, you will have to wait for the next meal, as I must treat Evans for his corn first, otherwise we won't proceed any further," said Taff One.

"In that case, I don't mind waiting," said Leader. "What treatment have you recommended for Evans, then?"

"First, I will have to operate on his foot, with a razor blade that I found," said Taff One.

"As there is no anaesthetic, I will hold him down," said Leader.

"If this is going to hurt, I'd rather have the corn. I'm getting quite attached to it, anyway," said Evans.

"It's not going to hurt," said Taff One. "Come over here while the light still holds."

He placed his throbbing foot on the stone slab which Leader had wiped clean.

"Operation commence," ordered Leader.

"Stop before you start," Evans said.

"Don't be such a frightened bunny, remember that you have been trained to stand pain and other discomforts," said Taff One.

"The Atomic Army did not at any time mention corns, or say that I'd have to have natural surgery without the aid of painkillers," said Evans.

"In that case, you will have to visit a chemist and obtain one of those corn bandages that are now available," said Leader, who had picked up this information from a woman's magazine he had read, but hadn't told the others.

"Let's have a look at your corn, Evans. It's a bit shiny for a corn. No wonder it hurts, it's not a corn at all, you've picked up a drawing pin in your foot."

"Pull it out, Taff One," said Evans.

"There might be a loss of blood when I do," said Taff One.

"I'll risk it," said Evans.

"Well, here we go then, you hold his foot, Leader, while I do the tricky bit," said Taff One. "One, two three, here it be."

"Phew! That feels better already," said Evans.

"Better try and hop on it as soon as you can," said Leader. "Here we go then, hop, hobble, hop, hobble, hop, hop, hop!"

"Thankfully, I seem to be back to normal," said Evans.

"Surely, it must now be time for eats," said Leader. "I'm starving, and a hungry leader is not a happy leader."

"I'll hop off and get something," said Evans, and off he went, doing skip hops and double skip hops.

"There doesn't seem to be much wrong with him now, does there," said Taff One.

Evans returned, laden down with water cress and some whortleberries; these were served up on plates made from dock leaves, which could also be eaten, to save on the washing up. To drink, he produced a bottle of spring water, which glistened when it was poured.

"That's much better," said Leader. "Park the tandem by that bush over there, and we can sleep on a pile of dried leaves, that should keep us warm and comfortable until morning. If we all sleep with our feet touching, then we won't be able to hear each other snore, and we'll wake up refreshed and ready for the next stage of our journey."

They spent a most comfortable night, and Leader was awake first, owing to his nose being tickled by a leaf-end.

"Morning, campers," was Evans's greeting to the world. Taff One just grunted a fairly loud rabbit grunt, squeaked and stretched.

"Another glorious day," said Leader.

The Atomic Army was inspected and awarded good marks for a good turn out. Breakfast was eaten: a mix of groundsel and elderberries, all enjoyed it.

"Get the map out, Evans," said Leader. "We must find out our exact position before we are able to proceed any further. We must be nearing the S.A.S. training area."

"I don't think we are near Hereford yet," said Evans.

"Well, we'll see when we check the map," said Leader.

"Here we are. We seem to have by-passed Knighton and are here at Mortimer's Cross," said Evans.

"Does anybody know why he's cross?" said Taff One.

"Who?" asked Leader.

"Mortimer," said Taff One.

"Do try and be quiet, Taff One, otherwise you might not hear the correct instructions for avoiding the S.A.S. at this crucial stage," said Evans. "The question now is whether we cut into England, to Leominster, then Hereford, Ross-on-Wye and on to Chepstow, or do we stick to the safer route of Hay-on-Wye, Pandy, Abergavenny, Monmouth and then Chepstow?"

"I think we'd better call another meeting of Atomic One," said Leader.

"I hate meetings," muttered Taff One.

A meeting was convened and all were present, in body if not in mind.

"Which route shall we take?" asked Evans.

"I would like the easy route," said Taff One.

"We would all like that, but neither of the routes will be at all easy," said Leader. "Which is it to be?"

"I think we should go to Hay-on-Wye," said Taff One.

"What about the king there? He might have troops at his disposal," said Leader.

"I hadn't considered that," said Taff One.

"You must take all things into account," said Evans. "You suggest the route, Leader."

"Well, if it's up to me, I suggest we cut into England and pass under the very noses of the S.A.S."

"They will not be expecting that," said Evans.

"True, very true, very, very true," said Taff One.

"That's it then, we will go where the danger is most apparent. All in favour," said Leader.

"Yes," said Evans.

"Yes, I suppose," said Taff One.

"Proposal carried; any other business? No! Meeting closed."

The three climbed aboard the tandem and started to pedal towards Leominster; the road was fairly straight and passed through many picturesque villages with a few old fashioned shops. The three pulled up at a sub post office-cum shop, and made a few small purchases. The proprietor asked if one of them was named Evans.

"Why do you ask that?" asked Leader, ever watchful.

"There's a card here for an Evans," he said. "It arrived yesterday."

"Well, as a matter of fact, his name's Evans," said Taff One.

"Would that be Atomic Evans, by any chance?" he asked.

"Well, yes it would," said Evans.

"This is for you, then," he said, giving Evans the card.

"Thank you," said Evans.

"Who is it from and what does it say?" asked Taff One.

"You can guess who it's from," said Leader.

"No, it can't be. Yes, it is; it's signed 'Aunty Flo'," said Evans.

"How does she know where we are and where we are going to be?" asked Leader. "How does she know?"

"What does the card say?" said Taff One.

"It says, *Be very wary as you pass through Hereford, there are many dangers there. Best of luck to you all - signed Aunty Flo,*" said Evans.

"Well, at least she's to the point this time," said Leader.

The Atomic Three pedalled on until it was dusk, when they snatched their last meal of the day.

"Have you noticed that it is getting very much darker, very much earlier, these nights?" said Leader.

"I've noticed that it's getting colder at night," said Taff One.

"When we reach Hereford, we will have to resort to burrowing at night, for extra safety," said Leader.

"I hope that does not mean we will have to get in touch with the burrow surveyor," said Evans.

"No, we won't have to do that, because we are on a secret mission," said Leader.

The Atomic Army were travelling less and less miles, owing to the shortening of the days, and it was the end of October when they approached Hereford.

"Did you see that army camp we just passed? That was S.A.S. headquarters," said Evans.

"All I saw were signposts which said NO PHOTOGRAPHS, was that it?" said Taff One.

"Yes, it was," said Leader. "We will have to be extra vigilant for the next two days."

It was beginning to get dark, and Leader picked a spot to dig the burrow for the night, a quiet night with not a sound, not a movement, and the Atomic Three slept soundly and very snuggly.

The only give-away to their plan was the tandem and sidecar parked at the entrance to the burrow. The next day passed with a lot of pedalling and sparse meals. That night they burrowed again and just as they were finishing the dig, all hell was let loose - an S.A.S. attack. Missiles, explosions and many lights lit up the sky. The attack went on for about an hour. The Atomic Three dived into the dark, furthermost recesses of the burrow. Trembling and with teeth chattering, Leader asked if everybody was O.K. Evans replied that he was. Taff One didn't reply, as he had his eyes shut and his paws in his ears and both his legs crossed for luck.

"Give him a shake, Evans," said Leader.

Evans shook Taff One.

"What's up," said Taff One.

"Leader's asking if you are O.K."

"Yes, I'm fine. How are the rest of you? That was a narrow squeak, we can do without too many of those," said Taff One.

"Better poke your head out and see if the tandem is all right," said Leader.

"Why me all the time," said Evans.

"Please carry out orders," said Leader.

Evans very gingerly poked his head out of the burrow. The tandem was still where they had left it.

"Funny that," thought Evans, as he went back down the burrow and reported it to Leader.

"That is very strange. Perhaps they have booby-trapped it," said Leader. "We'd better not touch it until daylight."

Morning at last arrived, after a long, uneasy night for the Atomic Three. All three crept out of the burrow, to inspect the tandem for hidden devices and secret wires; none could be found.

"Now, that is very strange indeed," said Evans.

"I wonder what the S.A.S. plan is," said Leader.

"We'd better have something to eat, or there will be nothing of us left to fit into any S.A.S. plan," said Taff One.

"You're right, Taff One. Better try and find breakfast."

The Atomic Three searched, and all they came up with were some rose-hips and acorns.

"Not very appetising," said Evans.

"Better than nothing," said Taff One.

"I think we'd better make a small purchase at the next shop," said Leader, "just to supplement things, you understand."

The Atomic Three boarded the tandem, and had travelled for about two miles, when they approached a shop.

"Go and buy some vegetables, Taff One. Here's the money," said Leader.

Taff One hopped off the tandem and hopped into the shop; he reappeared, five minutes later, with a big cabbage and a stick of celery.

"That's better," said Evans.

"I've some news for you two," said Taff One.

"What is it now?" asked Leader. "Aunty Flo can't have

written to you as well."

"No, better than that, Leader," said Taff One.

"What is it, then?" asked Evans.

"The attack by the S.A.S. last night was not an attack," said Taff One.

"Don't be stupid. Why were all those missiles and explosives used on us?" asked Leader.

"It wasn't against us," said Taff One.

"Who was it against then?" asked Evans.

"It was against no one. You see, it was November the fifth, Guy Fawkes night, so we need not have worried, it was just bonfire night."

"Well, thank heaven for that," said Leader, "but that does not mean that we will have to be less vigilant in future. Anything could happen on a journey as perilous as this."

"Anyway, that was very good news, it shows us that the S.A.S. do not know our whereabouts, at present, anyway," said Evans.

"Come on, let's get to the next lay-by and share out this cabbage and celery. I'm starving," said Leader.

Chapter Nine

Off they went, for what seemed like miles, until they spotted a lay-by at long last.

"Pull in there, Evans, before we all conk out," said Leader.

They ate the cabbage and crunched the celery and felt a lot better.

"Now for our push to Ross-on-Wye," said Leader, "we must try and reach there by tomorrow night."

"I think we'll do it with ease," said Taff One.

"I just hope that we arrive there in one piece, that's all," said Evans.

The Atomic Army stopped for dinner and tea, but were finding it more and more difficult to find the correct balance of foods, and were having to rely more and more on the berries in the hedgerows.

"I don't know how people get hooked on vitamin C. I'm going off it completely, with all these berries we are eating," said Leader.

"The light's fading fast now," said Evans. "Why don't we purchase two lights, a white one for the front and a red one behind?"

"That reminds me, could we have a softer seat at the back," said Taff One.

"Always thinking of your own comfort, that's you, Taff One," said Leader. "We'll have another think about it in the morning. First, we have to dig a burrow for the night, and let's try and hide the tandem, just in case."

"Use those ferns over there," said Evans.

The three then had an easy dig and produced one of the best burrows they had dug for a long time.

"Now to get some hay in the bottom and we'll be very snug," said Taff One.

They all went down for the night, feeling delighted with a job well done. It was very warm down in the burrow and, as nobody could get to sleep, a competition was suggested. Each had to tell a story, which could be true or false. The best story would then be judged, and voted to be true or false, and the winner would receive the honour of riding in the sidecar for the rest of the journey.

"Who goes first?" asked Taff One.

"You can, if you like," said Leader.

"I think that's a pretty stupid idea, anyway, I don't know any stories," said Taff One.

"Well, that knocks another idea on the head," said Leader.

"I don't know about you, but I'm going to sleep," said Evans. "Good night."

With that, they managed to nod off until morning; Leader was pleased that he didn't have to vacate the sidecar.

It was raining when they awoke, and everything they touched was clammy, wet and cold. It was not a good start to the day for the Atomic Army, but one they had been trained to deal with.

"Let's stay down the burrow until it clears up," said Evans.

"That's a good idea," said Taff One.

"Oh, very well, but only until it clears up," said Leader.

"What's to eat?" asked Evans.

"Nothing much, I'm afraid, just some roots that are growing down here," said Leader.

"I hate roots," said Taff One.

"They are not top of my list of gourmet foods either," said Evans.

"Then I suggest that we proceed with due haste to Ross-on-Wye, for a full breakfast," said Leader. I'm paying."

"I think that's worth getting my ears wet and my fur damp for," said Taff One.

"You're right there," said Evans.

They went up to the surface and uncovered the tandem, pointed it at Ross-on-Wye, mounted it and pedalled through the rain, headed for the first café to serve full breakfast.

Ross-on-Wye turned out to be a very pretty town with friendly inhabitants. Even the traffic wardens smile. They parked the tandem in one of the long stay car parks, and now that the rain had stopped, the Atomic Three felt that they could wander about and take in a few of the sights. During the day, they had a number of cream teas, and Taff One was getting to be quite plump again. It was time to push on for Monmouth, but first they had to remember which car park they had left the tandem in.

"Better ask someone where the long stay car park is," said Leader. A lady was walking up the road. "Go and ask her."

"Excuse me, Miss, but could you tell us where the long stay car park is?" asked Evans.

"I'm sorry, but I'm from New York, in the U.S.A. You will have to try somebody else."

"There's a workman coming along, ask him," said Leader.

"Could you direct me to the long stay car park?" asked Evans for the second time.

"Well, there are more than one in Ross," said the workman.

"Oh, dear, we'll never find our tandem at this rate," said Evans.

"The best advice I can give you is to go and ask in that

office over there - The Tourist Advice Bureau."

"Good afternoon. Could you give me a list of long stay car parks in Ross, please." I've not only lost our tandem, but I've lost your car park, too," said Evans.

"Well, what did it look like?" asked the lady.

"Oh, it had two wheels on one side and a sidecar with one wheel on the other," said Evans.

"No, not a description of the tandem, a description of the car park," she said.

"Well, it was a flat piece of ground with a lot of cars in it," said Evans.

"I didn't mean that," she said. "What I meant was, were there any outstanding buildings near this car park which you have managed to lose for us?"

"I don't know. I didn't notice any," said Evans.

"In that case, we'll have to direct you to the two nearest and hope for the best. Go out of here, take the first left for two hundred yards, the first car park is on your left; if that is not it, carry on right for another two hundred yards. The second car park is on your right. If neither of these are the one you are looking for, come back and ask again," she said.

"Thank you," said Evans. He went down the road and took the first left, then on for two hundred yards, to the car park on the left. What do you know! There it was, the long lost tandem.

"Goodbye, Ross-on-Wye. Here we come, Monmouth," said Leader.

Off the Atomic Army went, whistling an ancient rabbit tune as the last light of autumn began to fade.

It was three days and nights later when they reached the outskirts of Monmouth; the only problem had been a shortage of ready food. If it hadn't been for the scrumping skills of Evans, the Atomic Army would have been very down, both physically and mentally.

"Monmouth has a castle," said Taff One.

"Is that what that big building over there is?" asked Evans.

"I don't think we'll stay there tonight. You can't get in, anyway, as it's run by the National Trust, and they have a system of times for opening and closing, and it's well past closing time," said Leader.

"Thank goodness for that. I certainly did not want to spend another night in one of those draughty, eerie castles," said Taff One.

"Where shall we spend tonight? I don't feel like digging a new burrow tonight," said Evans. "It's much too dark, anyway."

"Why can't we stay in a hotel for a change?" asked Taff One.

"No, that's not the answer, and it would deplete our funds even faster than they are disappearing already," said Leader.

"Well, where are we to spend the night?" asked Taff One.

"The next vacant house we come to - it's over the wall and into the garden," said Leader.

"That looks a likely one, over there," said Evans.

"Yes, that one with a FOR SALE notice in the grounds," said Taff One.

They steered the tandem up to the gate, dismounted and had a quick glance over the fence.

"Look over there. There's one of those greenhouses," said Leader.

"That's it then, into that. It looks a bit cold in the light from the moon, but at least it will be draught-proof," said Taff One. "I just hate draughts."

The greenhouse was unlocked and the three pushed their way in.

"This seems comfy," said Leader, pushing himself under the staging. "That's it, then. Heads down, tails in the air, see you all in the morning."

With that, Leader went off to sleep. Evans was just about to doze off, when a voice was heard to say, "I can smell lettuce."

"Go to sleep, Taff One. You can smell lettuce in the morning."

"They all dropped off. When they awoke they saw a wondrous sight: a row of lettuces all running to seed.

"Whoopee! That's breakfast taken care of," said Leader.

The Atomic Three munched through as much as they could, and Taff One was about to get his head down again when Leader said, "We must have a new strategy to cross over the Bristol Channel."

"Why do we need a new strategy?" asked Evans.

"Well, we cannot cross the Severn Bridge in daylight. It would be much too risky," said Taff One.

"Correct," said Leader, "and just another point: they don't allow bicycles or tandems to cross, anyway."

"How are we going to cross, then?" asked Evans.

"I suggest that we try and cross with the tandem at three in the morning; this is the time when there will be very little traffic about," said Leader.

"A good idea, Leader," said Evans, "but won't there be a man in the hut, collecting tolls. He might notice that it's a tandem."

"I've thought of that. We don't have any lights on the tandem, and if we keep in the shadows, he might not notice, especially when the glare of the toll booth will be against a dark sky."

"You seem to have cracked it this time, Leader. I only hope you are correct," said Evans.

"Well, do we all agree with that?" asked Leader.

"Certainly do," said Taff One.

"And I do certainly," said Evans.

"Good. That's settled," said Leader.

"Let's make our way to Chepstow as soon as we can," said Taff One.

"Why the hurry?" asked Evans.

"I'd like to call in and see my cousin Un," said Taff One.

"You've never mentioned him before," said Leader.

"I'd forgotten about him until you mentioned Chepstow," said Taff One.

"It's funny how, when you join the Atomic Army, there is always something to look forward to," said Evans.

Monmouth was now fading into the distance as the Atomic Three pedalled on. Another meal passed by. Meals were beginning to become very plain, with none of the fresh, succulent juices from the various plants that had been in season, but onward they must go, enduring the hardships that were coming their way.

They reached Chepstow at long last. Now to find Cousin Un and, with a bit of luck, have a party to rejoice in the meeting of long lost friends. Taff One made enquiries at a few local burrows, and was told that Un had just returned from holiday and could be found at Green Meadow - south of Chepstow. Off the three went, and arrived at Green Meadow, to be met by Un.

"Hello, Un. I hope you remember me - Taff One," said Taff One. "It may be *un*dignified of me to remember, but you must know how *un*excitable I am on these occasions," said Un.

"Thank goodness, I would not have liked to be treated as a total stranger," said Taff One, "especially by a cousin."

"That would have been *un*deserving," said Un.

"And if that had been the case, it would have made me very *un*happy, Un," said Taff One.

"Never mind all this drivel. Can we stay here tonight?" asked Leader.

"You *un*doubtedly can," said Un.

"We will try and make it an *un*forgettable event," said Evans.

"How about some *un*washed carrots and a lettuce or two for supper," said Leader.

"That menu was *un*foreseeable," said Un, "but I'll do my best." With that, he disappeared down the burrow *un*accompanied. He reappeared with the goodies and said, "I hope this will go some way to quell those *un*satiable hunger pangs of yours,"

"Well, it's bound to help, Un," said Evans, casting an eye over the food.

After supper, the three tried to entertain Un by singing some *un*familiar rabbit songs, then it was time to go down the burrow that Un had given them for the night.

"Good night, Atomic Three. I hope your slumbers go *un*disturbed," said Un.

The Atomic Three thanked him and went below for the night. Un went to look at the tandem, and thought, "I suppose it is *un*oiled. I'm *un*sure, but I'll oil it, anyway." Un found some fresh oil and did the best he could, as he was quite *un*mechanical, when you got down to it. He was *un*talented as well, but he did try his best.

All had a good night's rest, and wandered around Chepstow on the following day, looked at the sights and ate the occasional green plant. The Atomic Three did not rest that night, but made their way with the tandem down to the Severn Bridge. They bade goodbye to Cousin Un, and were *un*sure of things to come, but they waited quietly for Leader's signal, at about three in the morning.

Time passed very slowly, as it does when you are waiting for things to happen. At long last, it was time to make a move. The Atomic Three mounted the tandem and made their way to the toll booth.

"How much is the toll?" asked Leader.

"Forty pence a car," came the reply, in a familiar voice.

"I knew it," said Evans. "It's our other cousin, Jacques, who was captured with us by the S.A.S."

"What are you doing here, and why have you given up

selling onions, Jacques?" asked Taff One.

"It's a long story, mon ami, but it keeps the sheep in the meadow," said Jacques. "How long have you three had a car? The last I remember was that you had a tandem and a sidecar."

"Well, to tell you the truth, we still have it, and before you say that we are not allowed to cross the bridge with a tandem, we know; but the Atomic Army must return to the retraining area as soon as possible," said Leader.

"In that case, I, Jacques, will make an exception this once, but only because there is no traffic about and we are cousins."

"Thank you very much, Jacques, we will remember your great kindness," said Evans.

"I, too, wish to thank you," said Taff One. "Ta, ever so, Jacques."

"It is nothing, but please hurry across the bridge, and do try to cross with speed and stealth," said Jacques.

The Atomic Three pedalled as hard and fast as they could and managed to clear the bridge with no incidents happening and without being spotted by the S.A.S. It was now time for self congratulation and a morning in bed, to get over this latest success in the journey to Wookey retraining centre.

The Atomic Three slept on, and only awoke because the rumbling of their empty tummies was getting unbearable.

"Evans, it's your turn to find our next meal," said Leader.

"Not me again," said Evans.

"Oh, do hurry up, Evans. I could eat a giant cabbage all on my own," said Taff One.

Evans hopped out of sight and was missing for a long time; so long, in fact, that Leader and Taff One very nearly called a meeting of Atomic One, but had to decide against it, as there were only two present, and to call a meeting, all three had to be there, to form a quorum.

Evans returned, pushing a wheelbarrow, well, not so

much pushing as hop-pushing, a method he used to conserve energy. The wheelbarrow had an assortment of eats aboard - cabbages, swedes, turnips, lettuces and a bunch of Italian grapes. There was one other item, an invoice for the above goods, with a handwritten note at the bottom that said, '*A discount of 10% if paid within seven days*'.

He passed the invoice to Leader, who grunted, "There goes some more of our funds. Couldn't you acquire the eats by looking in the countryside?"

"Very sorry, Leader, but we seem to be in a built-up area, and the local market seemed to be the answer to our immediate problem," said Evans.

"Don't be too hard on Evans, Leader. We are all very hungry," said Taff One.

"How much is this invoice?" asked Leader, as he looked at it. "Eighty-seven pence less ten per cent. Now let me see; that's a saving of eight and a half pence, which brings it down to seventy-eight and a half pence - not as bad as I thought it would be."

"I'll go and pay the invoice as soon as you give me the money, Leader," said Evans.

"That's sorted out, then. How about transferring the food from that barrow to our tummies, before we forget what food tastes like," said Leader.

The Atomic Three had a banquet and emptied the barrow in an eating event that had to be seen to be believed.

"I'm too full to move," said Taff One.

"And so am I," said Evans.

"We must never get into this state again; what if the S.A.S. were to attack now! We would all be captured," said Leader.

"Perish the thought," said Evans.

"If we sleep this meal off, we should be back to our active selves," said Taff One.

"Is that your answer to everything: just to get your head

down?" said Leader.

"We may as well, we're too full to do anything else," said Evans.

"Well, just this once, and that's final," said Leader.

It was snooze time at temporary headquarters for the Atomic Three. Four hours passed by, with them in this state of collapse. It was now well past midday and the sun was high in the sky. Taff One awoke, followed by Leader. Evans slept on.

"Pull his ears, Taff One, that should do the trick," said Leader.

Taff One did as he was told and pulled Evans's ears. Evans awoke with a start.

"What's up?" he asked.

"Well, the sun is up for a start, and Leader expects you to be up and about."

"No dinner today," said Leader. "Get yourselves aboard the tandem."

The Atomic Three were once more on the move.

"Remember to read the road signs, all of you; we don't want to go through a city centre," said Leader.

The Atomic Three were so intent on reading signs that they didn't notice a furniture van, with the back down, forming a ramp, which they rode up. They were at the far end of the van before anyone had noticed.

"How did we manage to do that?" asked Taff One.

"I thought we'd come to a tunnel," said Evans.

All of a sudden things went dark, the back of the van had been closed.

"Well, we seem to be in a right pickle now," said Leader. "We are trapped in this van, and we are also without food."

The engine of the van started and the van began to move off.

"Where to now?" asked Evans.

"I don't know the answer to that one," said Leader.

"I want some food," said Taff One.

"I've told you already that we are without food," said Leader.

"O.K., brain, what be your next question?"

"I think we'll have to hold a meeting of Atomic One urgently," said Evans.

Another meeting was called, and all were present and all were mobile. Taff One spoke first, "Help! What is going to happen?"

"We don't know that," said Leader. "Let's start with what we do know."

"I think we'd better," said Evans.

"We are trapped in this van and the van is on the move, we don't know where to at present," said Leader.

"Perhaps we'll have a better idea when we stop and they open the back," said Taff One.

"That must be the understatement of the year," said Leader.

The van lurched to the right, then to the left, then right again. A screech of brakes, and the van came to a halt. The back of the van went down and the van was filled with light. It had stopped outside a depot for other vans of a like kind. A big sign above the yard gate read, "PACKERS THE SHIFTERS - CHEDDAR".

"There we are, we are in Cheddar, not too far away, so let's creep out of this van and make our way to Wookey."

The Atomic Three slipped out of the van and left the yard; back on the road, things were again beginning to look a little better, and the excitement sharpened when they reached a signpost which had "WOOKEY HOLE" on it.

The Atomic Three stopped and foraged by a stream for food, and were quite surprised by what was growing and in a good, edible state. They once again filled up their tummies. Leader noticed that everyone was happier after they had had something to eat.

The next village was, indeed, Wookey but, as it was getting dark, the Atomic Three made camp for the night.

Morning came and the Atomic Three fell in for their last inspection before getting to the retraining area. They were all turned out in a very smart manner and were complimented. They made their way via the signposts to Wookey Hole.

Taff One was the first to reach the building, and he hopped back at a rate of knots, his face white with fright.

"Leader, I have some bad news to report. The S.A.S. have been here before us and have decapitated all the workers and villagers, and put their heads on shelves in that building over there."

"Oh, dear, Atomic Army on Red Alert," said Leader.

The Atomic Three went into their crawly position and made their way very slowly to the building. Sure enough, there was the line of heads placed on shelves - a very gruesome sight.

"Just a second," said Leader. "Those are wax heads; this is a sort of museum."

"S.A.S. attack, my foot," said Evans.

"It could have been," said Taff one.

"We are very fortunate that it was not," said Leader.

"Where are the officers who are going to retrain us?" asked Evans.

"It is very strange," said Leader.

"Well, I haven't seen anyone that faintly resembles an officer," said Taff One.

"Look over here, Leader, on this notice board."

On the board was pinned this notice:

ATOMIC ARMY NOTICE 1A

DUE TO FINANCIAL CONSTRAINTS, THE ATOMIC ARMY IS TO BE DISBANDED, AND ANY FUTURE OBJECTIVES ARE TO BE POSTPONED AT PRESENT. THIS DOES NOT MEAN THAT THE ATOMIC ARMY CAN RELAX. MEMBERS MUST KEEP THEMSELVES FIT AND VIGILANT AT ALL TIMES, IN CASE OF EMERGENCY. HEADQUARTERS WILL INFORM EACH MEMBER INDIVIDUALLY OF ANY FURTHER OPERATIONS, IF AND WHEN THEY OCCUR.

Signed

Commander-in-Chief, ATOMIC ARMY

Aunty Flo.

"Well, that's a turn up for the book, that is," said Leader.

"What do we do now?" asked Evans.

"That's all very well, posting notices. I'm going home, for starters," said Taff One.

"We'll join you, if we may," said Leader.

"Let's get back down the valleys. I've had enough of this, anyway," said Evans.

The Atomic Three hopped quietly north, headed for the Welsh valleys. They whistled rabbit tunes as they went.

"By the way, Leader, what is your correct name? You cannot have been born with a name like Leader," said Taff One.

"Well, it's Rowley, actually," said Leader. "What's your first name, Evans?"

"It's Alan," said Evans.

"That leaves just you, Taff One. What's your first name?"

"I don't mind my first name being known to you both. It's Leonard."

So, there we have Rowley, Alan and Leonard.

"That means our initials are R.A.L.," said Evans. "Rabbits Are Lovely. Isn't that nice!"

ATOMIC
ONE
MEETING
IN
PROGRESS
LEADER
EVANS THE MAP
TAFF - ONE